Fringe Dwellers

Stories of People Living on the Edge

Fringe Dwellers
Stories of People Living on the Edge

Shane Joseph

Second Edition

Hidden Brook Press
writers@hiddenbrookpress.com
www.hiddenbrookpress.com

Fringe Dwellers:
Stories of people living on the edge
by Shane Joseph

Editor – Jake Hogeterp
Cover Photograph – Federico Serrano
Cover Design – Richard M. Grove
Layout and Design – Richard M. Grove

Typeset in Garamond

Printed and bound in Canada

Library and Archives Canada Cataloguing in Publication

Joseph, Shane, 1955-
    Fringe dwellers : stories of people living on the edge / Shane Joseph.

ISBN 978-1-897475-44-7

    I. Title.

PS8619.O846F75 2008   C813'.6   C2008-906339-2

Introduction

When I began assembling the stories that comprise *Fringe Dwellers*, I realized that my characters were normal but damaged individuals. I did not have a Fagin or a Kurtz to distort reality. I therefore wondered at the time whether this collection would be dismissed as mundane.

However, as I commenced my readings and toured the land, and the first readers began reading these stories and giving me feedback, it occurred to me that I was connecting with my characters in real life. Almost everyone I met had experienced a twist in the road during their life that had led to deep revelations about themselves. I found people willing to stand up in public and say, "Hey, I too am a Fringe Dweller – here's what happened to me..."

It takes only a moment, a gesture, a false step, to send us out into the margins from a position we have toiled all our lives to build. And it can take an eternity to return to base, if at all a return is possible. But in recovering ground lies the spiritual learning that transforms. It was these journeys of my characters that I attempted to capture in this book.

Therefore, as this second edition comes out, I offer it not only to those living on the fringe but to anyone who has experienced a life-defining moment, who believes in second chances, and who is convinced that giving up is not an option.

Shane Joseph
2010

Contents

1

Fringe Dwellers

The old man first came into the coffee shop three days after we opened for business. My daughter Amina was behind the counter with her mother, while her older brother Roshan served tables marking time until he could scoot off to hockey practice. For me, it was a time of rushing, trying to get everything in order. I had always worked at a desk job; this new one, of constant movement and multi-tasking, was draining. Still, it made me proud to be working after months of fruitless job hunting.

He was old, but a big man. He walked with a limp and wore a torn, oversized coat. His grey beard was scrawny; long matted hair under an old beret gave the impression he'd just woken from a nearby alleyway. I saw Roshan making his way over, pointing to the "No Loitering" sign that my wife had been so insistent upon. "Huh, we came from a good class in India; no going down further in life than we have to." Opening a coffee shop was bad enough for her; catering to derelicts was pushing it too far.

But before my son got to him, the old man pulled a crumpled

twenty-dollar bill from the folds of his shabby coat and plunked it on the table. Roshan looked back at me and I shrugged. Our customer was solvent; we could not refuse him service.

I served the coffee and bagel he ordered, while my wife wrinkled her nose. As I neared, I almost gagged on the rancid stench of sweat, reminding me of the beggars in India. It's funny; unwashed bodies all over the world expel the same odour. So much for cultural disparities – we are all one, at least in our filth.

"Good morning," I said, placing the mug and plate in front of him.

He grunted. And I thought Canadians were polite!

As I turned away, he said, "Why'd ya come to this country?" His voice was raspy, like that of a heavy smoker.

I looked back. He hadn't touched his coffee or bagel. He was staring at me.

"Ya hear me?"

"Why did we come? For the children, of course." That was my stock answer now, even to this bedraggled stranger. Why would a fortyish ex-civil servant with a BA in English from India, with no Canadian experience, and speaking in a funny accent, come to Canada otherwise? Believe me, I had tried everything to get a job. From cold calling, to mailing umpteen resumes, to attending the few interviews I managed to obtain. But I always got that same response, "Your qualifications do not quite match what we are looking for."

"For our children – Amina and Roshan" I said, pointing to them. I detected stubbornness in my voice that my wife would have said was out of character for me.

"For the children, eh?" He nodded as if that was a good enough reason, and started to slurp his coffee, dismissing me.

A busy spurt took my attention as a bus dropped off another horde desperate for its caffeine fix. "This is a good location – you will make lots of money," the previous owner, an immigrant like us who had come out ten years ago, told us. He was selling up and moving to Richmond Hill, having paid his dues to 'poor immigrantdom'. Yet his price was high, and it was still unclear how many customers we needed to break even. And what about weekends when public transit ran a skeleton schedule along our route?

Out of the corner of my eye, I saw the old man waving me over as I tried juggling a tray of used cups and plates left by patrons from two bus loads ago.

"So you came out for the children, eh?" was all he said. I noticed that the bagel was only half eaten and he was stuffing the remainder in his pocket.

"Can I get you more coffee?"

"No thanks!" He rose and a pungent gust wafted to my nostrils as crumbs popped out of the folds of his coat and strewed the floor.

"That's a very good reason, my friend – the children. They must never make the same mistakes."

He broke wind mightily before pushing through the door.

*   *   *

A few days later, I spotted him in the park that ran along the main road across from our shop. I was pushing a grocery cart loaded with the week's supplies, and dreaming of the day we could buy a second-hand minivan so I wouldn't have to do this fifteen-block trudge anymore.

There he was on a bench, throwing scraps of a bagel – probably the one he had bought earlier in our shop – to the pigeons fluttering around him. Beside him were paintings. Park strollers paused to peruse the artworks. He seemed uninterested in the passers-by; his attention was focused on feeding the birds. My curiosity was mounting, so I pushed the grocery cart into the park. It was a cold mid-December day, and he had an extra blanket over his shabby coat, and wore open-fingered mittens.

The paintings surprised me. They were scenes of war – horrific images of men dying in trenches, with the most ghastly expressions on their faces, and guts hanging from shrapnel-blasted wounds. Blood was splattered everywhere. In each of the pictures the horizon was full of blue skies – another world just beyond the mayhem.

"Fifty dollars each," he grunted without looking up.

An older man standing beside me handed over some cash and said, "I'll take this one, Sid. The others have too much sun and blue skies in them."

"Oh, that's how it's coming to me now. More sunshine. Less of the dark stuff," the man feeding the pigeons said. The other man put the painting under his arm and strode away with a, "See ya next month, Sid."

"Yeah, stay out of trouble, Charlie!"

"Hello there. I'm Vinod from the coffee shop. Remember me?" The man looked up and recognized me.

"Oh, you the guy who came here 'for the children'?"

"That's right. I didn't know you were a painter."

"Oh, I've been many things. That's what I do now – paint."

"I take it you fought in World War II?"

"That'd be right."

I was curious. I am not much of an art connoisseur, but I could tell the pictures were not those of an amateur. He had the right degree of shadow; the emotion etched on the faces reached out and gripped the viewer. Pathos tugged at my heart. Perhaps being transplanted in this country had made me melancholy. I wouldn't have paid any attention to a street artist back in India.

"There is real feeling in your paintings."

"When you've been there – you know. Wanna buy one? Give it to the kids – that way they won't go to war. None of them should ever go to war."

"It's too stark to put up in my shop."

"People put them up in their basements. Especially us ones who went into combat. Then they sit in front of them – often when no one's around. Helps with grieving, they say. Charlie's bought over a dozen of 'em since his wife died last year."

Fifty dollars was a lot of money for a frivolous luxury and I hesitated. He looked at me knowingly. A faint smile creased his features.

"Tell you what – it's late and I gotta be going soon. I just put up the 'half price' sign."

I couldn't refuse. I put the painting on top of my groceries and started to push the cart down the slope to the park gate. Just then, the cart hit a stone and slid out of my frozen hands, rolled ahead and overturned, spewing its contents on the pathway. I swore and started to gather up my damaged purchases – the eggs were goners and the bananas mush.

A hand reached out from behind me and placed the painting, which had been the first to fall, back into the cart.

"Ya know – you're at war too!" Sid said.

"What do you mean?" I retorted.

"Ya lost something when you came here. Now yer fighting to get it back."

When I got home, I got a shelling from my wife who had been waiting impatiently for the groceries, so she could get on with preparing lunch.

"Twenty-five dollars for that horrid painting? Vinod, are you out of your mind?"

Amina used one of her newly-acquired Canadian expressions, "Yeew Appa, it's so totally gross!"

"It was only to help a poor old man. After all, he's a customer," I insisted.

"You are both going 'Canadian' in very strange ways," my wife declaimed. "Amina, why don't you try speaking proper English for a change? All these Canadian words that don't mean anything!"

"Oh, Ammi – do you think we speak proper English, with our Indian accents and all?"

I left them to their language debate and made my escape, even though I shared my wife's point of view and would have liked to join in.

Roshan wasn't around to pass judgment on my purchase; he had skipped out the moment I arrived to practise in the alley with the new hockey stick I had bought him. He was determined to master this new sport called ice hockey and would occasionally look at the clutch of local kids who had a net up on a side-street in the next block. My wife often complained about the freedom I gave him to explore his new environs when he should have been helping run the family business.

I decided to place the picture in our flat above the shop, but very soon it was forgotten among the clutter that one buys in this country – parkas, boots, clothes, appliances, groceries – stuff that is hard to store in a cramped two-bedroom apartment already bursting at the seams with our belongings from India, which in this cold country, had also become junk.

*   *   *

Sid came into the shop often after that. Every time the same order – a cup of coffee and a bagel, half of which disappeared into his coat pocket. And he paid the bill, always leaving a fifty-cent tip.

One Sunday, when the buses were running only on the hour, and I had given the rest of my family the afternoon off to go to the mall, he came in. This was not his regular visiting time, and he looked disturbed and angry.

"Coffee and bagel?"

"Just coffee," he growled.

I let him settle down with his coffee, attended to other customers and then walked over.

"Something is the matter, Sid?"

"Damn government!"

"What's happened?"

"They won't leave me alone – that's what!"

He sipped his coffee in silence, while I tidied a nearby table.

"They wanna give me a medal – the bastards!" He slammed his mug on the table so hard I thought it was going to splinter.

"For the war?"

"Yeah."

"But that's good news, isn't it? Recognition after all these years? Your bravery helped Canada become the great country it is. That's what attracts people from all over the world."

"What about what they owed me, eh? Damn war took me leg, took me brain, took me family, took me fucking friends – how'd they pay me back for that?"

I was taken aback by his outburst and looked around to see if it had upset any of my patrons, but the last one had departed a few moments ago. We were alone in the shop and the next bus was not due for another twenty minutes.

"How old is yer boy?"

"Fourteen."

"Humph. We weren't much older. I faked my age at sixteen to get in the army. Was the thing to do – stop the bloody Nazis, eh? We fought all the way from Normandy to Bruges. There was boys like yer son dying all around. I was so sick I kept asking why I was not allowed to die with 'em. But oh, no, I was spared – so I could come back and drink like crazy to forget; put me pistol to me head and play Russian roulette; and still not die. I got married and had kids, thinking that would help. Frightened the wife out of her head. She and the kids left one day. That's when I stopped drinking. I don't even know what they look like now."

"Didn't you get some kind of assistance – from the Government?

"I don't want no charity from 'em – when all they gave us was a load of bull about serving King and country. I got me paintings and I'll keep working till I drop dead."

"Still, a medal is a great honour."

"My trophies are other things. Here …" He pulled out an old pencil from his coat and wrote an address on a napkin. "You come to my place sometime. I'll show ya."

* * *

The following Sunday, after I closed the shop, I looked for Sid in the park. The only sign of him was a faint trace of crumbs from his half bagel – even the pigeons had moved on to more lucrative scavenging elsewhere in the park. Taking the crumpled napkin from my pocket, I decided to chance my wife's wrath and visit him. I suppose I was trying to get involved in this country; apart from my changing family and the shop, Sid provided the only intriguing distraction in my new life.

The houses on his street ran out at number 42. His address, number 48, and the lots adjoining, were cordoned off by a huge white board fence. A notice, proclaimed in oversize letters:

Condemned Property

Chemical Seepage

Do not Enter.

A rickety gate led through the barrier into an open area with a couple of rusting cars, a pile of rotting garbage and a scattershot of debris. A pathway wound its way to a small garden shed, the type they sell at Canadian Tire. Twigs were burning in the hulk of a battered barbecue and Sid was sitting on an upturned crate, painting by the firelight. He coughed between dabs of his brush.

"Ya made it." he said, without looking up.

"You've got quite the place."

He coughed and rose. "Come." He pushed open the door of the shed. A camp bed and a side table with a tin mug and kerosene lamp stood against the opposite wall. Clothes hung from the rafters and various personal items filling open garbage bags littered the interior. The lamp threw eerie shadows over the room.

"Use the bed; it's the only seat I got."

I did as I was told and picked my way over, sitting down in spite of the nauseating staleness of the bed sheets.

He pulled a shoebox from one of the garbage bags and sat down beside me.

"These are my trophies."

He handed me a stack of newspaper clippings. They looked to be of various peace protests dating back to the fifties. There were shots of a younger Sid – hippie-style long hair, droopy moustache, a little leaner – being dragged out by riot police. In one news clip he was in handcuffs, blood all over his face.

"I protested them all: Korea, Vietnam, the Gulf War, Yugoslavia, Afghanistan – all of them. See! They always dragged me out. But not before I got a couple of punches at the party poopers. Boy, it felt so good."

"I don't understand, Sid. Why do they want to give you a medal now?"

"The last time I got arrested, they traced me history. Even had an article in the newspaper – here it is. And they found out what happened in Normandy."

"What happened?"

"I got separated from me mates and blew up a Jerry pillbox to save some American lads who were alongside on the beach. One of the GI's, who lives in Buffalo now, read the article in the Canadian newspaper, remembered me name and told the cops what happened. So they thought they'd give me a medal– the bloody fools!"

"That's a great story."

"Yeah but what they don't know is that medals don't end wars. Wars start other wars. It really starts when ya come back. The war in the head. When ya wake at night screaming; when the people around ya think you're crazy; when ya can't love anymore because you're all fucked up."

"Do you still scream at night?"

"Not as bad. Especially since I started painting."

"But you are still angry?"

He started putting the clippings away. "Aren't you angry?"

"Me? Why?"

"They never give you guys a chance. I seen them immigrant people come here – do all the shit jobs – why? Ya look all educated like. Ya even talk with all them million dollar words."

I was grateful for the shadows thrown by the lamp. "There are times when I feel that way. But I keep reminding myself that we came for the children and that makes it bearable."

"That's bullshit. I said that too. But you can't help the children if you're fucked up. They may get better jobs than you, but they'll be fucked up too."

Then he broke into a fit of coughing; I thought he was going to collapse. He staggered outside and took a few gulps of air. "It's me lungs – they get this way every winter."

"You should see a doctor. Now that's something this country has to offer – free medicare."

"Don't want no free medicine. Free medicine didn't save me leg – shrapnel's still in it."

His stubbornness was becoming tedious and I decided to bid him goodnight. When I stepped out of the shed, I glanced at the almost completed painting propped on the easel – the same old war scene; but even in the flickering firelight, there was no sunshine and no blue skies on the horizon in this one.

As I picked my way down the path his words kept returning

"You can't help the children if you're fucked up." Was that true of me too? Or was I in denial?

*　*　*

When spring came we bought the minivan, re-conditioned. We had to. My wife's sister's family – our sponsors – had introduced us to the more established circle of friends and relatives who had come to Canada years earlier. All were doing well; all owned property, and many had thriving businesses. Money – well, there was plenty of that floating around. And we had to keep up, even though that meant getting into debt like every other patriotic Canadian. When I tallied the bills, we were just breaking even on the coffee shop after paying ourselves a modest monthly income; but with summer coming, traffic was going to drop and things were going to look less rosy. I told my wife that I needed to go back to school to get a diploma in Business Administration.

"Vinod, are you crazy? How will we afford it? And who will mind the store?"

"Well you are the one saying that running a store is beneath our class. How can I ever emerge from this hole if I don't try something else?"

We fought over it. I approached a cousin - one of the rich ones - for a loan.

"You took money from Surendra?"

"I'll pay him back, when I get a better job."

"You'd better pay him back even if you have to sell the store. Can you imagine how they will talk if you default?"

I was weighed down by these difficulties late one Sunday evening in early summer. I'd just closed the shop and was sitting by the window – my favourite spot. Cash ledgers, entry forms for the college, GST refund forms and a myriad other documents that I had to put in order before retiring upstairs, were piled before me on the table. I heard a tapping on the glass. Sid was peering in at me.

I opened the door halfway. "Sid, we're closed. But you can come in and have a coffee with me if you like. On the house."

"No, no – didn't mean to disturb you. I see you are fighting the battle. Them papers look all important like. Just wanted to wish ya luck, whatever yer up to."

"I'm thinking of going back to college."

He started coughing. The cough had become deep and hollow now, as if there was nothing left to expel. "That's good. You show 'em, boy." Sid's face glowed despite his discomfort.

"And you take care of that cough."

"I'm going down to me old mate's cottage this summer. We were buddies in the war. Barney's the only one left now. Him and me."

I did fill out the form for the college that night. There was no sign of Sid at all during the summer. But I had other things to occupy myself. We went looking for houses. The down payments were staggering – a minimum of thirty thousand, and in the boonies (I was picking up new words too!) just to be able to keep up with our rich cousins.

"We will have to sell the shop to make the down payment," I said. Our entire life savings were in this little street-corner enterprise. "And then I would have to get a regular job to afford the mortgage."

"Or, I could work." my wife said.

"Yes? And who will mind the store?"

"You could get a temporary assistant, and make sure Amina and Roshan do their share."

"And I can't get even a shot at a good job here unless I have a Canadian qualification."

And so went the endless debates around the dinner table every night in our apartment above the coffee shop.

If your heart is set on something you eventually get it. So my wife got a job as a temporary office assistant and I hired a summer student to help out along with Amina and Roshan, who also were expecting to be paid now – it was the Canadian way. And as September came around I started my business classes. What I had not figured out was how to find enough hours in the day to run the shop, study, sleep, and allow for recreation. And as September moved into October, the strain started to show. My wife and I lost interest in sex, or going to the movies or the temple. All those other things we did as a family fell by the wayside as well. It was work, work, work – the Canadian way. But we were engaged in the battle – as Sid would call it – and when you are in that state, you don't think.

One night in late November everyone was asleep and I was plugging away at my studies, feeling that I was in too deep, when my eyes fell across Sid's painting. It was partially covered by Roshan's new Maple Leafs jersey that was conveniently hanging on the same nail – his mother's gift to him from her first paycheque. I tossed the jersey on a chair nearby, took down the picture and looked at the dying soldier. Somewhere along the line that young boy had nursed dreams like Roshan, like me, but they were never to be – death had come at the most unlikely time of life. And what was I worrying about? After some time, I felt better. I hung the picture back on the wall where I could see it every night while studying.

My wife's income helped us hire another assistant to tide us over the Christmas period. We got an added bonus too; as part of my course I had to come up with an innovative project and decided to open my shop window that fronted the bus stop, converting it into a "latte-to-go" corner. Within a month this nook was doing more business than the regular shop. Things were starting to look good, although we were no less busy.

That is why it took me until December 24, when everybody's last-minute Christmas preparations put an abrupt halt to business, to realize that Sid had been missing the entire autumn. He should have returned from his friend's cottage months ago. That night I felt compelled to drive down to number 48 again.

As I slopped through slush down the path from the rickety white gate, I heard moaning and quickened my step. The door to the shed was ajar and the kerosene lamp had all but flickered out. The coughing was weaker than I remembered. The blast of fetid air was stifling and I had to keep the door wide open. He was lying on the camp bed, buried in old blankets. A plate of smelly congealed soup mouldered on the side table. He was shockingly thin.

He opened his eyes and his whole frame shook upon seeing me. It seemed as if some giant monster was trying to break free from him. Then he began crying. "Barney… me mate died this summer, at the cottage." He cried shamelessly. Tears he had withheld for many decades. This big man was like a little baby in swaddling clothes – on Christmas Eve and all.

"We need to get you to the hospital, Sid." I was not taking no for an answer this time.

"No hospitals! I'm going this time… going with me mates."

"But you haven't got the sunshine in your paintings yet, Sid."

That pulled him up short and he even stopped sobbing. He peered at me.

"You're too bloody smart – you know that?"

"My van's outside and I'm not leaving until you come with me."

"I'm not coming." He pulled the blankets more tightly around him.

That's when I lost my temper.

"I may be stressed out Sid. But I'm not fucked up like you. You hear? I am not fucked up."

"Fuck you!"

"You're a burned out, pathetic man Sid. You think everyone's out to get you – well, we aren't you know."

"Maybe not you – but the others."

"What others – huh? Your fellow Canadians? Well, I am part of Canada now – whether you like it or not. This city is half-full of people like me. And I care. Otherwise I wouldn't be in this miserable shit hole tonight."

He glared at me; that was all he could do.

I got up and went to the door. "I'm going to my van; it's the white one parked outside the gate, and I'm going to wait fifteen minutes. If you do not come out by then I'm going to drive off and you can forget about ever finding the light in your paintings, and die like the rest of them. Goodbye Sid!"

It hurt me to leave him; but I stormed out, upset with myself, with him and with the whole bloody world for being so ungenerous.

I sat there, and fifteen minutes didn't seem to tick away fast enough. Maybe he was too weak to walk, but I knew he would not want my assistance in making up his mind. He had to do this on his own. I switched on the radio; Christmas music reminded me of peace on earth and goodwill to man. Sid and I had seen a different side of things. We were the fringe dwellers of this society: me wanting to get in; him wanting to get back. I switched the radio off and started the engine. The quarter hour was up. As I was about to release the hand break, I heard the coughing and a shadow moved. A limping, sick old man in an oversize coat was making his way over.

* * *

Sid was in hospital for over a month. He refused visitors and I stayed away at first. When I eventually went to see him, the nurse on duty advised me that he had recovered and released himself just the day before. She said, "He was a handful when he arrived, suspicious of everyone, refusing our help. Once he saw that the staff only wanted to help, he began to soften. He went out like a lamb in the end – just like the month of April." I went down to number 48 but the place was deserted. He didn't come by the coffee shop or sit in the park after that.

The following summer my wife's temporary job ended and she decided to restore work/life balance to our family by not seeking further employment and I was delighted. This was my last year of studies and I needed the focus; I was glad for her support back in the shop. Roshan was invited by the neighbourhood kids to play street hockey and he couldn't wait for those moments. He said he was also ready to try out for the school team this fall. Amina had decided she would never wear Indian clothing again – so un-cool, she said.

One hot August evening, I closed the store early – we had the financial latitude to do this on occasion now. My latte-to-go idea had been brilliant. I was sitting by the corner window doing the books. I discovered that if we operated like this until I finished my studies and got a decent job, we could sell the store at a premium, as it had higher revenue generation now than the last time it went on the block. The house in Brampton, that my wife had been alluding to, was within reach, even though we'd be in debt for the next twenty five- years – but who cared; it was the Canadian way.

A familiar tap sounded on the window and I looked up to see someone I could hardly recognize. The grey hair was combed and the beret gone. So was the beard and he looked years younger. He was wearing a short-sleeved shirt and khakis, but I sort of missed the baggy overcoat.

"Sid!" I opened the door and pulled him in. He hesitated on the threshold looking to see if we were alone. Then he sat down and let me get him a coffee.

"Where the devil have you been?" I asked.

"Oh, here and there. After I got out of the hospital they found me a volunteer position at the hospice. That's where I live now. Didn't know there were still kind people around."

"Great! Are you still painting?"

"Yes. But the paintings are kinda different now."

"I'd like to see them."

"I'll bring them by sometime. Nurses pushing sick people on wheelchairs in the sunshine and that kind of stuff. How's your family doing?"

"Still fighting our battles," I chuckled.

"But winning the war, eh?" he winked.

"Slowly… slowly. In about twenty five years."

"It took me a bit longer."

"That's why I am not impatient anymore."

Outside, Roshan and his friends whizzed by, rollerblading over to the next block to play street hockey.

"Why don't we go out and watch the kids play?"

Sid drained his mug. "Now that sounds like a good idea."

The sun was warm on our faces as we stepped out into the street.

*   *   *

Sid died five years ago. We have the house in Brampton; the kids are finishing university, and I did get that job as an analyst in a financial services firm downtown. Sid's painting lives on the wall opposite my desk in my home office, a place I seek refuge in from time to time, from work, family and other responsibilities. My wife also works; as an administrative assistant – a permanent position now. Once a year, among the many rituals I perform, I drive down to the cemetery in Toronto and place flowers on Sid's grave, and a half bagel so that the pigeons will keep him company.

2

Valentine Promise

She was in the public library, typing furiously on one of those new-model computers with flat screens. *What happened to typewriters?* She came here most afternoons now to keep up her skills.

"You say I am polished, classy
You whisk me away
It's Valentine's Day …"

A great opening, taking her to the time when she was a cheerleader and general joie-de-vivre of the class of '71, before her teaching career began. She felt inspired. Today was a magical day, when even the gods embraced romance and love. She looked forward to what the evening would bring and wanted to be bold.

"My martini's bright red
Just a touch dangerous …"

Oh, she'd been dangerous all right – in a nice way. Her petite blonde looks always turned heads whenever she entered a room.

An amateur ballroom dancer, her poise exuded grace and vitality. Men still paid attention and looked for a hint of promise in those vivacious eyes. But she was choosy. Her man had to have class, like her. The serial monogamist, she'd called herself: always faithful to the men in her life for as long as they had stayed with her.

But those men - or her judgment - had been flawed. Her only marriage ended after two years. A series of live-in boyfriends followed, each lasting an average of five years. They all left her in the end. Two of them died – one in a boating accident, and the other skied off a mountain, caused an avalanche, and was only found when the snow melted in the spring. If that wasn't bad enough, there was the one who fled with another woman; and yet another who went psycho and shot himself, failed to aim properly and lives today in a mental home with severe brain-damage. *Losers, all of them.* Yet she refused to lose faith that the man of her dreams was "just over that next hill." Entering her fifties, and having opted for early retirement, she was still looking for that dream lover.

"Amid rattan and plush couches
We sip cocktails, bodies touching …"

She had persuaded Jim, her new man, to take her out on Valentine's Day and Gloria was already mapping it out. *Keep a positive image in front of you and it will manifest itself.* Pity the men in her past had not shared that point of view. She hoped Jim would.

Jim was a writer – a thoughtful, contemplative man – who had recently lost his wife. They had found each other at a writers' workshop a month ago. They delighted in discovering associations between his prose and her poetry. The next time they met, he read her a short story he had written, based on one of her poems. "Gives it depth and breadth," he said. She loved it; loved what he could do with her words and symbolism.

"On the dance floor, we come alive
Your reflection in the glass, lithe, sultry
Hot and free
You mirror the music
Your pelvis rhythmic
In tune with Latin and Reggae
You lead, I follow …."

She had always loved to dance, twirling jives and vaulting tangos. She was not sure if Jim could dance; they hadn't been out yet. Today would be the first time. But he was reasonably athletic and of average height and weight; he should be able to move his pelvis. Maybe, she expected too much from her men; built them up beyond all reality only to lose them in bitter disappointment when they did not measure up. Fifty plus years on this planet and she had not yet learned this lesson. Is it wrong to expect the best in everyone?

Her eyes went moist and her pulse quickened as she typed in the next lines. The guy at the terminal next to her had the music on his portable CD player blasting too loud and the reggae strains of "Let's get together and feel all right" overflowed his earphones.

"The vodka hitting me
I lean against your shoulder
close my eyes and trust.
We move as one
Synchronized
Passion
fuelled by the heat of the music"

She needed to insert capitals in the right spots and place less emphasis in others – *Passion* – that warranted a capital P. The grammar check on the PC kept underlining everything: it did not recognize poetic verse. She needed help: computers and Gloria did not work well together. She had retired because of the new ways of work that had crept into the classroom – new attitudes of working to rules concocted by trade unions; it was not about equipping the next generation with literacy anymore. Passion had driven her work, not rules.

The assistant librarian – black, bright and young – just out of university no doubt, was in charge that evening. Gloria waved her hand and pointed at the computer screen. The assistant got up and walked over, looking at her watch. Her name badge read "Amanda Stevens".

"Need some help?" Amanda said.

"Yes. I have to get this done before closing time. But these funny lines say I am composing everything wrong. Is there something I am not doing here?"

"Let's see." The assistant leaned over. Gloria smelled the shampoo in the other woman's hair, and glimpsed her thrusting breasts through the front of her blouse. The freshness of youth surrounded Amanda like an aura, making Gloria sigh. *I was once like that. I had breasts that did not need bras and other props to hold them up. If only we had a second chance to fix all the wrong turns we took in life and access the fountain of youth again – without resorting to hormone replacements.*

Amanda fiddled with the keys. "I'm turning your grammar check off. This a long poem?"

"Only a page."

"Well, you must have done something. It's showing twenty

eight pages. If you hit 'print', we will have an avalanche of blank paper."

"Oh, shoot! I'm hopeless with these things."

"There, I've fixed your page setting. It's a pretty poem. Didn't mean to pry, I couldn't help but read."

"It's about a date I'm having tonight. This is how I want it to end. Are you going out this evening?"

Amanda frowned; then shrugged. "I guess so. My boyfriend is picking me up after work. Says he has a surprise planned for me."

"Aren't you excited?"

For the first time, Gloria saw the radiance of youth slip from her young companion's face. A pained expression replaced it.

"Benji is a musician. He does not last long in relationships, although he's lavish on surprises."

"Live in the moment, my dear. If he takes you out tonight, nothing else is important. One night, one moment; make it last a lifetime."

"I know his last girlfriend. She warned me about his short attention span."

"Well, maybe she is just a trifle jealous. How long have you been with Benji?"

"Six months. His ex said that's past his staying power."

"You'll be just fine. Lay it on thick for him tonight. Men are like pets. They need lots of loving to stay docile."

"You've scripted what could happen to you tonight. What if it doesn't happen?"

"Oh, it will. Trust me." *Focus on the positive, Gloria.*

"Well, I'd better get back. Watch that 'enter' button – could get you into trouble. We close in fifteen minutes. Do you think you'll be done? I've got to lock up after the staff leave. And I can't be late for Benji, can I?"

"Of course my dear, you cannot be late for Benji."

Gloria returned to her work. *Now to the last verse — the coup de grace!* She would give Jim the poem, just before he took her home from the dance. Then he would know for sure that she wanted to give herself to him tonight. Men his age were either too brash or too shy. She suspected Jim was the latter.

She gave the poem a once over and hit 'print'. Suddenly the printer by Amanda's desk started chugging out paper. It should have stopped at one page but kept on printing. Paper began falling out of the tray at the other end.

"Amanda — help! I think I've done it again!" Gloria was running towards the machine. It wasn't printing blanks either; multiple copies of her poem were spewing out and falling over the floor. A student in the vicinity started picking up the papers, and reading the contents, giggled. Other library users joined in to help while the printer kept going, reluctant to end its job.

Amanda rushed over, smiling. "Yes you have!"

"Please, I swear to you, I followed your instructions." Gloria had her arms full of paper and was thankfully retrieving more from her 'helpers'.

Amanda switched off the machine. "Maybe, there is a problem on our network. I'll have the technicians look into it tomorrow. Don't worry, I won't charge you for all this."

"Oh, thank you. Even the printer seems enchanted today!" When all the errant copies had been collected — there were over 50 this time — Gloria wanted to hold on to each one. Maybe she would present Jim with all of them tonight — show him how many times over she really and truly cared.

*   *   *

He stood outside the building. Another ten minutes and she would have to come out because the library closed at 5.30 p.m. Normally, he would have gone in – libraries and book shops could hardly keep him out – but today he refrained. He studied his reflection in the glass: medium height, greying hair with the top thinning, a little paunch accentuating the stoop of his shoulders, and now the thick lenses – he was definitely middle aged. *No kidding anymore, Jim. At least, Nancy won't be around to see you in your later years, when it gets really ugly.*

Kids skated on the ice rink nearby, and the snack bar was doing brisk business as mothers collected their frozen offspring coming off the ice and hurried them over for hot chocolate and other refreshments. The sun was going down on what had been a clear day; only the dirty snow banks on the edges of the community center complex reminded him of the last snowfall two weeks ago. He sat down on a bench facing the library doors. Another man, black, in his early thirties was pacing, talking into a cell phone. Scraps of conversation came his way.

"Yah man – we got the gig in Miami – April 15th – 2 weeks. Hold on. Another call's coming through. Hullo? Yah – I'll call you back. Bye. Elroy, you still there, man? Make sure you got the air tickets – five, I'm bringing Rita with me. What? Amanda? No, that's over – today… Yah, gotta go now. Peace bro."

The younger man was dressed in a black leather jacket and baggy pants. He paced up and down, plunked on the bench beside Jim, and shot right up again as if he'd sat on a bed of thorns. He resumed his pacing, dialling more numbers, talking to a myriad contacts. *Oh, to have the whole wide world in one's hand again! The preserve of the young.* Receiving a call back from his publisher was now an event for Jim.

The young man finally shut off his phone and put it in his pocket. He came over and sat down on the bench once more.

"Busy day, eh?" Jim said.

The young man turned with a start, as if surprised at conversation from a stranger. "Yeah, looks like."

"I was busy once," Jim said.

"You in the music business?"

"I was in business. Not anymore. Couldn't take the pace. I consult now – and write."

"Ah – a writer!"

"There's no money in writing. Even though it's my passion. That's why I consult on the side."

"Pleasure to meet you. Benjamin." He extended his hand. It was warm and clammy. "My friends call me Benji."

"I'm Jim. Nice to meet you too."

"You waiting for someone?"

"My lady friend. She is in the library."

"So's mine. She works there." Benji said. He got up and started pacing again.

"Would that be Rita – or Amanda?"

Benji stopped in his tracks and stared. He burst out laughing. "Hey, tha's out the frame, man. You was listening to my call!"

"Sorry, I couldn't help but overhear. You were rather excited. And loud."

Benji bit his lip and came back to the bench.

"You know what, man? I'm breaking up with Amanda today. She's the one in the library."

"Why?"

"Well, we've sort of reached the end of the line. I'm in the music business."

"I gathered."

"It's fast paced. I'm a rolling stone. My new girl is Rita."

"I gathered that too."

"What the fuck, man? You listened to ever'thing?"

Jim smiled at the younger man's consternation. "I told you, you were loud. I think you're pretty nervous too."

"Shit! It's always like this when I break up. It's tense, y' know? You ever been there?"

"My wife died. After twenty five years. I haven't broken up too often."

"Sorry to hear that bro – real sorry. My parents been married thirty five years. I don't think I can do that, man. Things move too fast in my life."

"Why did you wind up with a library worker then? Doesn't exactly fit with the musician image."

"I tried to slow down, man. Thought she would be the right one for me. But I gotta grab the breaks. This new gig is my first chance to play in the States. Rita has a condo down there. Met her at the audition. Amanda would not fit in down south."

People were coming out of the library now and lights were going off inside.

"They'll be here soon," Jim said.

"Listen, I don't even know you. And I've told you my life story."

"I'm used to that. I listen and observe. That's why I write."

"Your lady friend – is she special?"

"Too special. I don't think I can deal with her yet, though.

She loves to dance and I have two left feet. Besides, I'm still not over my wife."

"It's hard to break up – when you have to say goodbye."

"I never got a chance to say goodbye to my wife. She died in a car accident last summer."

'Man, I'm really sorry."

"It's all right. Why did you pick today?"

"It's Valentine's Day and I promised to take Rita out. So it's gotta be today."

"It will be brutal and cruel to Amanda."

"That's the only way you can make it stick."

"You are a cruel young man. You'll break her heart. Today, of all days."

"What can I say bro – live and let live."

"I understand. I'm breaking up with Gloria today too."

"What?"

"And here I am calling you cruel."

"But why the hell you doing that, man?"

"Yeah, I know what you're thinking. A man of my age should be lucky to have a date. Mark that well Benji – when you get to my age, you will not be doing what you are doing with Amanda."

"Then why are you breaking up, man?"

"I can't change women like you do. Like changing a pair of socks. I envy you for that."

"I told you. It's tense. But it gets better."

"You've had a lot of practice. I haven't. It's hard for me."

"Then why the fuck are you doing it?"

"Because I must love her first. I can't sleep with her if I don't love her. Maybe it's different for you, but I'm not into slugging for the homerun at the first at-bat. I took two years to fall in love with my wife. And we had twenty five years of bliss afterwards. Didn't look at another woman, didn't need to. Guess I am a slow burn."

"But you don't have to break up."

"She deserves better than me. Besides, I can't ask her to wait."

"Man, I think we both fucked up."

"We sure are. And there they come. If I am not mistaken that young woman closing the door behind Gloria is your Amanda? Good luck with breaking the news."

"You too, bro."

*   *   *

The fading sunlight leaves a magical crimson on the horizon. That moment of unreality before the darkness of night descends. A bird sits on the head of the gargoyle on the old building across the street from the community center. The scene plays out before its eyes.

The streetlights are coming on as the library lights go out. The last of the tiny-tots have come off the rink and are being hustled away by their moms. Maybe the moms have arranged for sitters to mind the kids, so they can go out with their husbands later tonight: after all, it's Valentine's Day, even for overworked moms. The snack bar is closing early tonight; perhaps old Joseph who runs the place has plans too.

Two women emerge from the darkened library. The younger one shuts and locks the door while the older woman, who is holding a sheaf of papers under her arm, strikes out across the square toward the bench by the ice-rink, where the older of the two men rises to greet her. The younger woman moves in the opposite direction towards the black man, who is walking away from the bench, as if he needs his own conversational space and privacy. They finally connect: two couples on either side of the rink.

After some animated conversation, both couples become contemplative, even sad. The bird leaves its perch, flies over and hovers. None of the four people pays attention to the creature.

"And I even bought a new dress for the dance," the older woman is saying.

"I'm sorry. It's hard for me. I spent 27 Valentine's days over the years with Nancy. I can't switch. I'll be miserable company tonight."

"But you have to let go …"

"I know. I need time. Besides I'm not much of a dancer."

She wrings her hands and looks about her, thinking. Then she hands him a piece of paper from the pile under her arm. "Here, I wrote this – for us."

"Thank you. I have to go now. Take care!"

She looks longingly after him. The bird hops over to the other couple and lingers.

"You need to grow up Benji." The younger woman is feistier. She is looking her companion in the eye.

"Sorry, it's not going to work out between us. Not right now anyway."

"Go on then. Go down to Miami and all those other places you need to get to before you settle down. And good luck!"

The younger man bows his head and walks away towards the parking lot. The younger woman turns back, tears in her eyes. She sees the older woman walking towards her, holding her head up and trying to look cheerful.

"You were wrong. The bastard ditched me," the younger woman says and starts to break down. The older woman puts her arms around her.

"Hush my dear. We expect too much from them, sometimes. We make them out to be more than they really are."

Between her tears, the younger woman says, "He had the balls to tell me that when he is ready to settle down, it would be with a girl like me."

"They're like puppies. We must love them. They need so much love."

The younger woman straightens up and looks in the direction of the older man who is walking across the square in the direction of the subway station. "I guess you had the same luck, eh?" She dabs at her eyes with a tissue. "Why do they pick Valentine's Day?"

"Yes, why do they? And it's happened many times before. I guess it's because there will be a lot of highs among men and women this evening, so there have to be few lows to level things off. We're the ones keeping the world in balance tonight."

The older woman glances over in the direction of the bird; it is busy picking crumbs left by the kids at the rink. Her face brightens. "I have an idea. We have a wonderful poem here that shouldn't be put to waste. Come with me."

The bird flies overhead, following the two women as they hurry down the street. Some of the mothers from the ice-rink are waiting for the bus with their kids. The two women start handing out sheets of the poem to the young mothers, and to anyone walking in the vicinity. Those who receive the papers, pause, read, smile, and thank the women graciously for their gift: couples snuggling closer together as they hurry on, the skating rink mums huddling around the bus stand to discuss the poem in a group.

"Thank you, Gloria," the young woman says when they have finally depleted their stock of giveaways. "You made my rotten day a bit more liveable."

"Go home, child, and be happy. You are young. Tomorrow, the sun will shine again."

The bird leaves them hugging goodbye and flies over to the parking lot where the younger man is beside his car, scratching his head. The bird settles on the roof of the vehicle. The man looks at the bird and suddenly makes up his mind. He dials his cell phone and, to his obvious relief, gets voice mail. "Hello, Rita? Hope you get this message. Can't go out today. Something's come up last minute. Sorry. I'll catch up with you soon. Ciao."

Then he quickly dials another number. "Elroy – yo brother – how's it hanging? Listen, make that only four tickets to Miami. Rita's not coming. Something's come up. Yeah. Listen, you fancy chilling with some beers tonight? Just you and me? No women! Okay. I'll bring over a six-pack. I need some serious chilling, man. I was wrong. It doesn't get any easier, the more you break up. I'm fucked up like crazy. See ya soon."

The bird follows his car as he peels out, tires whining on the slick pavement. Passing the subway station, the bird hovers for a while over the older man. He is seated on a bench outside, reading the paper the older woman gave him. The bird settles on the other side of the bench, just out of reach of the man. He reads the last verse out aloud.

"Next morning the bond is gentle.

We sip tea,

Content under the sheets

As sunlight fills the room"

Tears fill his eyes. "Ah, 'a consummation devoutly to be wished'," he says. "I wonder if I will even be ready by next Valentine's. Would my dear Nancy have finally departed by then? Or would Gloria have found another lover by this time next year – her man 'just over the next hill'?"

Then he sees the bird, perched on the backrest of the bench, looking coy, pecking the wood gently. He has seen this creature before, for he has known love and loss, and seen the bird appear many times since that hot summer day of the accident, when one too many glasses of wine had thrown caution out, and ushered death in.

"Ah, my little dove," says the man. "And what answer have you brought me today?"

But the night has fully descended. The time for magic is over and the man is left talking to an empty bench.

"Oh, no. You can't leave me without an answer!" For the first time this evening, he is angry. Angry for letting time go by in limbo, for living with ghosts of the past.

Ahead of him, the older woman is heading his way, bereft of her load of papers, head bowed, her poise still dignified. He knows that she will take the subway and ride off in the opposite direction, to spend the evening alone in her little apartment. He also knows now what he must do. The dove has spoken with its non-presence. He rises and goes to her.

"There is a coffee-shop across the street. Can I re-write this evening from the end of your poem and work up?

"What do you mean?"

"Will you be 'content to sip tea with me'?"

He has omitted the rest of the line –'under the sheets'.

But of course! She has so misread his readiness level. She has always done that with her men. That has been the problem!

"'As sunlight fills the room?' Oh, yes!" she says, smiling at last and holding out her arms to him. *Magic does happen on Valentine's Day after all. Even if it's not quite as you imagined!*

3

Beggars

Katie gurgled and spat in the drain that ran along the southern end of the big box mall. The cough was getting worse these days, and her clothes smelled so bad she did not raise her arms too close to her nose. But the grimier she was, the better it was for business. Her collection today – groceries, some old books from the giant bookstore, a couple of hot dogs from the vendor who had been in a generous mood – lay in a garbage bag beside her, next to the coins in her fiddle case. Sitting next to a garbage bag was lucrative; people felt sorry and doled out more. She needed a cigarette, but Pierre had taken the pack with him. He was working the other end of the mall; she would stroll over later. They chose not to be seen together too much as it might give the game away.

Pierre did not like her playing the fiddle when she worked; but it kept her mind active and her spirit preserved from the drudgery of begging. So to keep him happy, she did not bring her fiddle every day. He was right, she made more without it; besides she could move around and play many roles – opposite the supermarket for handouts of cash or a can of pop; or by the bookstore for a coin or a used book to read on the subway back home. She played her best act at the gas station across the road where she wandered among the pumps asking for money "because her car had run out of fuel on the highway". But the gas bar manager was on to her now so she had to be careful.

A coin dropping into the fiddle case reminded her to stash some away soon. No sense showing how rich she was. "Got a cigarette, mister?" she asked the truck driver who had just been generous. He had fished out a pack and was lighting up. She had seen him come by here often and he always gave her a coin. He turned towards her; his squat frame and grey hair reminded her of her father after a shower, when the soot from the mine was washed away. The truck driver's eyes were faded as if he had lost something in life and he spoke with the cigarette clenched between his teeth, puffs of smoke punctuating his sentences.

"You sure you want to smoke these coffin nails?"

"We're gonna die anyway. I'd rather die with my nicotine fix."

He offered her his half-empty pack. "Keep it. I'll get another one." He threw her a box of matches too. It had "Macy's Transport" written on it.

"Thanks mister. You from around here?"

"From Windsor. Where are you from?"

"Much further. A little town near Edmunston."

"That's far. My route takes me through there sometimes. Why are you here?"

"Came to make it big in the city."

"You're still trying to make it?"

"I'm on my way, mister."

He looked apologetic, as if maybe he'd stuck his nose in too far. "Well, take it easy. Gotta get some rest, myself. I have a long ride ahead." He strolled back to his truck and she saw him push back the seat and slump into it, pulling his cap over his eyes.

She packed her fiddle; time to find a new spot. Her grandmother's favourite proverb "a rolling stone gathers no moss" came to mind. That's why Grand-mère had lived in a camper and travelled all over the Maritimes, making home wherever she parked for the night. "I have the protection of angels," grandma said. Her father had stayed put in the mines, until the accident down in the shaft permanently buried him. That's when Katie had decided to hit the road and get out of small town New Brunswick and follow in her mother's (and grandmother's) footsteps. Her mother had left after the last of Katie's five siblings was born, and was never heard of again. On the train into Toronto, Katie had met Pierre.

Pierre was seven years older and from Nova Scotia. This was his second stint in the big city. He'd dropped out of school, come to Toronto five years ago and got mixed up with a gang of drug dealers. A deal had gone sour; a knifing followed and Pierre had hightailed it back to the Maritimes. He told her that he had found a new, risk-free gig in the big smoke and was heading back – and would she like to join him? It was thrilling to tag on with this wild-eyed young man with shoulder-length hair who would protect her from the unknown. That night he took her to a motel just off Guildwood station on Kingston Road. "Where all newcomers to Toronto hang out," he said. It was cheap; Pierre had an in with the management. Foreign accents seeped through thin walls. They drank cheap whiskey he had pinched from an LCBO down the road. Then they had sex – she for the first time. It left her feeling empty, but she shrugged it off as a rite of passage – it had to happen sometime, though she wished it would have been different.

Begging – that was Pierre's new business. And it was a business. On good days they could make over a hundred dollars each. Rich people in Toronto had money to spare. Pierre had staked out the new box store mall opened just off the highway on the east end of the city and invited her to work it with him.

"But I want a proper job," she said.

"You ain't gonna get one. In this place, university grads start in the mailroom."

And he had been right – she had tried several places for jobs – even the fast food joints were looking for "maturity and customer-service experience, with tertiary-level education preferred." Reluctantly, she decided to join him in his new profession.

"Don't call it begging. It's income equalization," Pierre said to bolster her spirits. When the pickings started to look good she wrote to her grandmother's post office box, saying that she too had found an angel. In Toronto.

Shaking off her reverie, she decided to stand outside the supermarket. She caught her reflection in the window. Dark hair cut short to boyish length, an oversized sweatshirt hiding small breasts and hanging down to her knees which protruded through torn jeans. Her slight figure had been an asset on the gymnastic team in school; now with the dirt and ravages of life on the street, it gave her an emaciated look in line with her chosen profession.

Customers were going in and out of the supermarket and business was brisk. This was not one of those no-frills places, but one that attracted an affluent clientele. Affluence, however, did not come with generosity — not always. There was the woman whose car was being broken into by a gang of teenagers the other day. Katie had intervened by throwing a stone and charging at them. Begging she could stomach; thieving she could not. The teens scattered in fright; but when the woman came out, she only saw Katie coughing from her recent exertion and hovering around the vehicle. Instead of thanking her, the woman shooed Katie away with a muffled, "Bloody beggars," under her breath. *So much for gratitude!* When Katie told Pierre about the incident, he marked the woman. On her next visit to the mall, the woman was surprised and anguished to learn that her tires had been slashed while she was shopping.

"Got some change for a bus ride home?" Katie had different punch lines for different days and even different times of day. But today, she had competition from the scrawny kid on the other end of the double doors with his scout uniform and carton of chocolate almonds selling at an outlandish price. So she took out her fiddle and pitched into a melodious "Danny Boy" every time the doors disgorged a clump of customers and their overflowing shopping carts. The kid glared at her and stomped away to find another niche. She thought about her twin brothers Jerry and Joe. They must be about the kid's age. She wondered what they were up to now, with no one to look after them. Probably separated and in foster homes. She'd have ended up in one too if she hadn't left home when she did.

"You play beautiful music." It was Tim, another regular who hung around the mall. Tim did not beg however; he was a retired telephone company employee, who suffered from a wasting muscle disease. Now he spent his days collecting receipts in the store so he could turn them in for cash with the supermarket management.

"Bon jour Tim! Ça va? – how's the back?"

"A bit better. This chair doesn't help. But I got lots of receipts today. Glad I came out." His girth spilled out on all sides of his battery powered wheelchair.

"I can come over and rub your back again."

Tim lived in the condominium down the road. One day, when he was in extreme pain, Katie had dodged Pierre and gone with the old man to his apartment, helped him onto his bed and massaged him for an hour. Tim had moaned in relief, and did not take advantage of the situation – like those dirty old men back at home who flashed at her on the way home from school. She felt she could trust Tim; not even Pierre could be trusted at times. In return for her hard work, Tim had given her twenty dollars and some lasagna from his fridge.

Tim's voice disturbed her thoughts. "Oh, that would be lovely. I've got some chocolate cake – we could have tea afterwards."

"Maybe tomorrow?"

"Did you think about what I told you the other day?"

She lit a cigarette from the truck driver's pack and inhaled in silence. She coughed. "Yeah. Not sure I could survive the course – what'll I live on?"

"There is government assistance."

"Not so sure Pierre would go for it."

"Remember, it's your life. Will you come tomorrow, then?"

"Okay. Merci beaucoup, Tim. Take care."

The old man threw her an endearing smile and steered his chair towards the crosswalk.

Different people reminded her of times past: the school kids who hung around the bookstore in the afternoons, smoking (she had picked up the habit soon after her mother left); the bum who staked his turf on the other side of the parking lot with the paper bag hiding his bottle – like all those people back home who hid behind booze to mask the emptiness of their lives (her father had been one of them); the cops who came by occasionally forcing her to stash her things and "mingle". Cops had come to her home the day her father died in the mine accident – they had brought the bad news. Even now they always represented bad news. Pierre was an anchor in this fluid world with which she had lost connection. Even though he squandered most of their takings on booze, he gave her a roof over her head at the motel, opened her to the needs of her body, and always made sure that there was food on the table. He protected her against the predators that hovered on their rung of the social ladder – the junkies and pushers who hung around the motel after dark. But he was also keeping her from progressing. Tim had suggested registering at the technical school to learn to become a call center agent. There were dozens of these facilities opening up from Kingston all the way to the Maritimes and with the bilingualism that came naturally to her, she could be an asset to any call center, Tim had said. He had also given her several addresses and references – his telephone company had hired many graduates from these training centers. She'd have to talk to Pierre – when he was in the right mood.

She packed her things and moved again. Across the parking lot by the entrance to the mall, a solitary, haunting figure dressed in a parka and with a scarf across his face, stood immobile holding a cardboard sign that read, "Please spare some change – Sick and need to get back home to Halifax." Pierre's latest gig – he didn't talk and couldn't be recognized in that outfit, and the more still he stood, the more attention he attracted, and the more change fell into the can by his feet as cars turned into the mall.

She signalled and the figure nodded – that meant another fifteen minutes and he'd be done. This was peak shopping time. She lit another cigarette and sat down on a patio chair displayed outside the hardware store. She counted her change – not bad – seventy four dollars and thirty eight cents – plus the half pack of cigarettes, book of matches and the contents of the garbage bag. She bit into one of the hot dogs; she'd keep the other one for Pierre. The sausage had gone soggy but she forced herself to eat. Smoking wrecked her appetite; sometimes she went a whole day without eating.

"How was the take today?" Pierre was at her side, bundling his costume away.

"Medium."

"Fuck!"

"Medium's good mais non, mon cher?"

"I got fuck-all at my stand. Got to change the routine."

"You gonna try the gas station round?"

"No – the fucking manager is on to me."

"Maybe this gig is blown."

"No. We've been at it less than a year. If we leave now, others will move into our turf. It's all about turf, honey."

"Am I really your 'honey'?"

He looked at her. His dark eyes creased in a smile. "You know I'm your guy." But his eyes didn't mean it. "Get the money out, let's pool."

He'd made only thirty-one dollars. "Fuck" he said when he saw her contribution.

"Hundred bucks a day between us is pretty good, Pierre."

"Not enough. Those creeps downtown are pulling in three hundred easy."

"But you'll get killed there, no? You told me that."

"I'm gonna get some booze."

He took seventy-five dollars from the collection.

"That's a lot for a drink." She wanted him to admit that he was now into crack on the days he fucked really hard and didn't seem to want to stop. She liked sex but not when he went on and on and on; and the next day he'd be grumpy and grouchy, and she'd be sore.

"Shut up. There's enough for dinner. Go get us something before the mall closes. I'll meet you here in an hour."

She made a grab for the money and he smacked her. "It's my money too!" she cried.

"You need me baby – don't forget. What I say goes."

"Since when?"

He smacked her again, not seeming to care if anyone noticed. A hardware store employee averted his gaze and ducked into the store. She felt humiliated. Until now he had smacked her only once or twice in the heat of sex and it had helped him come. And she had put up with it then because it was over sooner. Better sore cheeks than sore insides. But out here it was demeaning.

"Fuck you!" she said and stalked off.

He was laughing after her. "Remember, back in an hour – right here, honey."

She sobbed as she entered the supermarket. The pain in her chest intensified as she was wracked with a violent bout of coughing. She paused to catch her breath. She had cried a lot when she left home, but these past months on the streets had hardened her. Yet it was humiliating to be smacked like that. Pierre was getting really desperate now.

She stood at the checkout, with a carton of milk, a loaf of

bread and a packet of sausages. The cashier, a newly-arrived Asian girl, with dark skin and sporting a tag with "Hello, my name is Rani," was trying to explain to the old lady at the front of the line that the pasta was not on special. The customer was fiddling with her hearing aid, obviously not understanding. The cashier persisted until the old lady erupted, "What the devil is going on – can't anybody speak English?"

Anxious to get going, Katie intervened and interpreted. By listening to people talk as she begged, she had developed a flair for accents. The old lady nodded and departed muttering, "I don't know what this country is coming to."

The cashier smiled gratefully as she bagged Katie's purchases. Katie paid with a fistful of coins and went her on her way.

She stepped outside to wait for Pierre. Sitting on the steps she lit a cigarette – *damn, only three left.* She coughed with every puff now and tried not to inhale. She would have to stop this bloody smoking soon, before something bad happened. But, shit, it was so hard to quit. She fumbled through her pockets for Tim's piece of notepaper. She had carried it for three weeks, unable to decide whether or not to take the plunge.

As she was stubbing out the cigarette, she noticed the cashier sitting on the bench at the far end, surveying her. She was probably on a break.

"Thank you for helping," the cashier said in stilted English.

"No problem. She was an old bag anyway."

"You live here?"

"Down on Kingston Road."

"We lived on Kingston Road also when first coming to Canada. In a motel."

"Me too. I know the feeling. It's not the greatest."

"You live in motel too?'

"Yeah."

"What you do for job?"

"This and that."

"Do you beg? I see you many times in parking lot."

"Listen – it's none of your business okay, what I do."

"Please don't get upset. I have begged also."

"You have?" Katie was curious. "Where?"

"Back home. In Sri Lanka. When the soldiers came to kill us. I begged for our life."

"Oh! Must have been tough."

"Very tough. They still shot my brother and… and raped me."

Katie looked sharply at the woman – she must be a few years older. "What did you do?"

"When the soldiers were sleeping, our neighbours came and rescued me, we escaped to Colombo, and then to Canada. We were refugees here."

"Must be tough."

"I can never beg now. You don't need to beg here – everything is available. Why do you beg?"

"My boyfriend got me into it. It puts bread on the table."

"My boyfriend runs a grocery shop – Sri Lankan food. He helps me to go to night school. We are engaged. Next year we will be married."

"What are you studying?"

"First I study ESL – then I am going to do accounting. Tax preparation. It's a good business."

"Begging's good too." Katie said and looked away. She really hated Pierre now.

"I've got to go now," the cashier said. "Thank you for helping with that old woman – she was rude, no?"

"Yeah – very rude. See ya! I've gotta go too." Katie stubbed out her cigarette and pulled out Tim's list again. She tore a sliver of paper from the bottom and wrote a small note to the crippled man. As she folded the paper she saw a police cruiser drive into the mall, on its regular patrol. She went back into the supermarket and dropped the note in Tim's receipt collection box that he left behind the cashier's station. Hope he picks it up tomorrow, she thought. *Pity I won't see him again. But I will write.*

The police cruiser was parked outside when she left the store. The cops usually went in for a coffee at the donut shop, hung around a bit and drove away, missing all the action in the process – like when those teenagers tried to break into the snobby lady's car. She took a deep breath and walked over to the vehicle, trying to appear casual.

"Officer," she said, peering into the passenger side. "Wanna bust a pusher?"

The two cops looked surprised, even annoyed that they might have to do some work when all they needed was a smoke and coffee. "What do you mean, ma'am?"

"See that guy in the hood coming through the mall entrance? He's a pusher. I'll bet you a hundred dollars he's got stuff on him."

"What's your connection with him?

"I just know. Wanna bet?"

"Let's check him out," the driver signalled his buddy and the cruiser swung out silently, heading towards an unsuspecting Pierre returning from his "errand".

Katie lit another cigarette, taking in the scene as if she were watching TV: the police car closing in, the startled look on Pierre's face as reality dawned, his stumbling to escape, the siren going off as the car picked up speed, the corralling of the fugitive – Pierre wedged between the parking lot wall and the cruiser, with one of the cops frisking him – and finally the slow, forced-march back, to be thrust into the back seat of the car which took off with tires squealing. Through all this action she had not coughed once.

* * *

Katie stood on the grassy shoulder of the exit ramp to the highway flagging down vehicles. This had been one of her begging acts, assisted with the cardboard sign that read, "Student. Broke – trying to get home to Edmunston." Then, everyone had wanted to pick her up, not give her money. Now she had no sign; she was merely putting her thumb up to hitch a ride; yet no one stopped. A woman driver even spat out of her window, spraying Katie in passing.

She lit one of her two remaining cigarettes. The cough did not come this time either. Strange. She fished Tim's crumpled paper from her pocket again, trying to memorize the details. But her thoughts were distracted. Even though she was glad to be rid of Pierre, he had been her first lover. Now she was alone and that was the hardest part. She hoped it would not be long before she found another guy, a kinder guy. Come to think of it, the only real thing Pierre had been good for was sex – when he wasn't violent about it.

Her life in the Maritimes did not exist anymore; and now, neither did the one in the mall. The future was a big question mark. Despair hovered, threatening to engulf her. What if she flunked the course? What if she did not get government assistance? Then she pulled herself up – *stay focused!* But her courage ebbed. She prayed. Just as grandma said, the angels had been around her today – that Sri Lankan woman was definitely one. Tim too. But not Pierre. "The angels always come when you are at your lowest," grandma had said. "They watch over me dear, just as they will watch over you." But just at that brief recollection, Katie's euphoria washed away in a wave of hopelessness. She started coughing again.

As a big tractor trailer pulled up the ramp, her angst turned into full scale panic. *Why not just jump in front of this thing and end it all?* Just like Daddy in the mine shaft – one moment he must have been grumbling to his buddies, blaming the government for the plight of miners; the next a shudder and a rumble and a passing away into oblivion. But there was one difference; Daddy hadn't sought his end, however drunk and miserable he was. He had always looked forward to coming out of that mine at the end of every day and taking a shower before settling down with his bottle.

A squeal of brakes and a familiar voice shouting from the cab brought her back to the present. "Wanna ride, miss?"

She looked up. Macy's Transport, it said on the cab's door. Her friendly driver was looking through the window. "I'm not going as far as Edmunston, but I can take you somewhere close."

"How about Kingston?" She was shivering with relief.

"Sure, hop in."

"Merci!"

As she stubbed her cigarette and got into the cab, Katie could have sworn she heard the fluttering of wings.

4

The Librarian
and the Professor

He looked aristocratic, from a different part of the world, foreign and mysterious, yet sad and detached. He glanced at her during those odd moments when she passed the research section, where he was found surrounded by books, notepaper and a few curious students. She did not mind his furtive glances, in fact she was flattered. Who else gave her a second look in those days? Aristocratic, that's how she remembered him when he first knocked at her office door five years ago, following the advertisement she had pinned on the notice board at the library. He had been about Jack's age too.

"It's an annex on the lakefront, just behind the master cottage my late husband and I built. The rent is seven hundred and fifty a month over the summer."

"Just what I need," he said. "Three months to write my book. The one I've wanted to write all these years." He had an Indian accent; yet an Oxford education had dulled its edges and made it easier on the ear.

She would visit the cottage on weekends and see him next door. He drove a minivan, which carried all his worldly possessions – a PC, several books, some cutlery and crockery, a large musical instrument he said was a kind of a sitar, and a small bag of clothes. In fact he did not care much for his appearance, spending that long summer in flowing white or off-white shirts and jeans, his thick, greying hair getting longer and finally ending up in a pony tail. Yet his carriage and confidence prevented him from looking like a bum. His presence around the property started to grow on her quickly.

On sultry afternoons, when she sat on the dock by the boat reading, he would emerge shortly after two o'clock in running shoes and jogging shorts and take off along Lakeshore Drive, returning about an hour later, lathered in perspiration. Then he would head down to the water by the dock and do deep-breathing exercises for fifteen minutes. In the evening, sad sitar music wafted over to the master cottage where she would be rustling a solitary meal, too tired to go into the town, or not wanting to hear any more sympathetic sighs such as, "and Jack was so young… fifty-two… such a pity." Often, while tending the roses that were going wild, now that Jack wasn't around to help, she would see her tenant through the open window, working at his PC; he would get up and pace, then return to the machine, sometimes staring off into space for long intervals.

One day she received a mild shock. Returning to the cottage with groceries, she stopped off at the annex with the newspaper she had offered to get him, as he had been pre-occupied with his PC all morning. She tapped on the door but got no answer. Peeping in with a loud, "hello," she stiffened. He was standing on his head propped up against the far wall. He was naked from the waist up (or was it down?). His shorts had bunched up around the crotch, outlining the shape of a large penis and big testicles bursting to be free – ground zero of her stunned and startled gaze. The clock ticked as her face reddened to blushing-bride crimson. A speedboat roared by before they came out of their respective freeze-frames. He quickly uncoiled from the wall and straightened up with an apologetic look, reaching out for the familiar white shirt to cover himself. "Sorry. Yoga. It helps uncover the creative blocks."

*　*　*

She wondered whether she was prying too much and tried to stay away. After all, he was a tenant, and tenants were owed their privacy. But her own life was a wasteland. Jack had passed away only the year before from a cancer no one could associate with such a healthy man. Three months and he was gone. What a waste and a shock. Now here she was, a widow, not quite fifty, the opportunity to have children sacrificed to the exigencies of twin careers – he in public service, she in the library sciences. Her friends had advised her to try the dating scene again and a couple of months ago she had placed a tentative foot forward. But three disastrous dates with jaded men intent only on sex – and devious sex at that – had put her off. Her job as head of the university library in Toronto had sustained her during the grieving. The cottage provided refuge on weekends, but it also brought back memories of the happy times she and Jack had spent together. Therefore, she had been hoping to alter the cottage scenery somewhat, perhaps take in a tenant now and again. That's when Professor Ram Lal, newly arrived contract faculty member and professor of Afro-Asian philosophy, decided to approach her in response to her advertisement.

She researched his credentials before accepting him – the weirdos on recent dates had made her cautious. His past was sketchy: born and educated in India, post graduate degree from Oxford, professor in Nigeria for many years, immigrated to Canada ten years ago. Any other information was scant. On campus he was known as the taciturn one.

She did not go up to the lake the following weekend. Instead, she busied herself with city activities. There was the Mozart concert downtown and the new movie about Iris Murdoch's life. She envied Iris – free spirit, determined to make her point in a masculine world, satisfying her innermost desires and cravings, and yet having a loving man to care for her right to the end of an eventful life.

The following Friday, she took some lieu time owed, and returned to the cottage around mid-day. At first glance she thought he had vacated the place, barely halfway into the lease. The annex looked deserted and the minivan wasn't in the driveway. By evening she was pacing the living room, periodically glancing out the window towards the lake. When headlights finally broke the mist outside, her heart leaped.

When she heard steps on the gravel path and a tap on her door, her mouth went a trifle dry.

"Oh, hello Mrs. Jackson – Anne – you are back?" He was standing on her doorstep, looking as relieved as she was, holding a parcel in his hand.

"Good evening Ram – Mr. Lal."

"Do you like chapattis? I bought you some from the city." Jack and she had often enjoyed Indian food down on Gerrard St.

She invited him in, a little eagerly she thought. She wondered how Iris would have done it. He stepped across the threshold tentatively. "I really shouldn't stay."

"Stay at least and share this meal with me," she tried to sound matter-of-fact, but came across as pleading. And he obliged.

Later, they sat outside on her deck and looked out onto the lake, stomachs satisfied with the spicy food and glasses of iced tea hitting the spot, while the aromas of chapatti and sambar lingered in the cool misty air,. She was beginning to feel mellow.

"Did you drive to Toronto, just to buy Indian food?" she asked coyly.

He laughed. "That was one of the reasons. Actually, my daughter is getting married soon and I had to see to some arrangements. I am trying not to get too involved in these things these days."

"You have a family!"

"Yes. My son is already married. He is a computer engineer in Ottawa. My daughter is just finishing her Master's."

"That's a great accomplishment."

"Thank you."

"And your wife …?"

He took a sip of his iced tea. His glass was almost empty.

She reached for the pitcher. "Do you want some more?"

"No thank you."

They sat in silence. The mist had thickened on the lake. Soon they would have to go indoors. She was dreading the next step, unsure where it would lead.

"How's your book coming along?"

"It's a struggle."

"They usually are." She was relieved he was talking again. "I tried to write once. All I ended up with were short stories and poetry."

"Poetry is nice. I wish I could write poetry."

"What are you writing about?"

He paused for a long minute, then drained his glass.

"Desire …"

Her palms began to sweat despite the cool air. The seriousness of his tone as he uttered that word was chilling. She shuddered at a sudden bizarre image of him naked, with enlarged loins, sweating and breathing deeply by the lake over her suntanned body as they made love to sitar music.

"Desire is the cause of all suffering. That's what my book is all about."

He got up and gathered the plates. "May I wash the dishes?" She was too flustered to reply and merely nodded. He went indoors. She heard him washing at the kitchen sink and still hesitated going inside. She heard the slap of the front screen door. In a moment she saw him coming around the side of the cottage back to the deck.

"Thank you for the company tonight, Anne," he said. "You are very kind, and you have beautiful eyes. Do one thing. Please look up the meaning of one word in the library next week — Brahmacharya. That may explain things. Goodnight!"

* * *

She decided to cook traditional English fare that Sunday evening and brave a Monday morning run back into the city. There was Yorkshire pudding, her mother's favourite, and bangers 'n' mash, her father's indulgence from his military days. After all, Ram had been to Oxford, he should appreciate her cooking. At noon, with the pudding in the oven, she stepped over to the annex. He was typing away at his PC as usual.

"I wonder if you would like to come over for dinner tonight?" she asked.

A frown crossed his face. She decided to be bold in her rising panic. "It's time for me to return the favour from Friday night."

"I'm not sure. I have to get this chapter finished and it's the hardest part. Besides, my daughter may call me this evening." He didn't look anything like the man who had complimented her on her eyes only a couple of days before.

Excuses, excuses – served her right for chasing a man so unashamedly. "Well, there's plenty of food, I've been cooking all day!" He was torn, and she knew it. *Serve him right too! Would Iris have done this?*

By seven o'clock, she had showered and changed into a pretty floral dress, one that did not accentuate the emerging middle age spread. She lit candles around the dining table and put on Burt Bacharach. She opened the bottle of Californian Shiraz, although she did not know if he drank alcohol. This was her cultural experience, though; he'd just have to accept it graciously. Then she switched on the porch light and waited, taking a preliminary glass of the red wine to calm her nerves.

At eight o'clock, into her third glass, she decided to walk over to his side of the property and tell him what a coward and a cop-out he was – just like all the other men she had met since Jack's death. She downed the glass, shut the oven off – to hell with the food, let it get cold for all she cared – and stumbled down the path to the annex to tell him what for.

The wavy sitar music hit her dulled senses and she paused unsteadily on the porch, hand upraised to pound on the half-open door. There was a plaintive cry, a pleading in the sad notes. She peered inside.

There he was in the center of the studio-like room, a bed off to one side, table and PC off to the other; nothing between – all very neat and tidy. Seated on the floor in only his shorts, the sitar in his arms was like a baby being rocked to sleep – yet its music was transmitting from his very soul. He was wracked with sobbing and every shudder of his body was flowing into the instrument and emerging in the form of wailing music.

The effects of the wine evaporated quickly and she stood there, unseen, locked into his sorrow, feeling the same loss. Jack had died, but she had never really expunged the grief. Now this music was drawing it out of her. This half naked, tormented man in the center of the room was pulling at her every heartstring as he drew on the strings of the sitar. It was frightening to admit, but he was cleansing her.

She couldn't remember how long she stood by the door that by now had swung fully open in the gentle breeze coming off the lake. Finally, spent from his outpouring, Ram Lal slumped over the instrument, and was silent. She backed away and nearly fell down the steps. She staggered back to the master cottage, feeling weak, yet free of the anger with which she had arrived.

Then she cried and cried as had Ram moments before. It was a powerful, almost sexual release. He had touched her emotions in a way she had not anticipated. She finished the remainder of the Shiraz and felt fabulously light headed. She staggered about the kitchen, gulping handfuls of the Yorkshire pudding and bangers to quell the huge appetite that had suddenly welled up inside her – just like a post-coital pig-out; something she and Jack had often indulged in. Finally, satiated, she staggered into her bed and fell asleep fully clothed. "Thank you, thank you, thank you," was all she kept muttering, before falling into a dead sleep; something she had not had since Jack had taken ill.

*　*　*

"Brahmacharya" – the act of sexual renunciation or celibacy. She didn't find it in the Canadian dictionary, but in an encyclopaedia dedicated to religions and philosophies that had emanated from the Indus Valley in India over the last three and half centuries. She spent the whole week reading up on the subject. It gripped her to the point of obsession. Renunciation of desire was the prescribed way to end greed, wars, and other conflicts in the world. Gandhi had practiced it; Jesus Christ too, although he wasn't a Hindu. "Desire is the cause of all suffering," was a phrase uttered by the Buddha, another adherent. And now Professor Ram Lal was embroiled in it – and writing a book about it too. She wondered what desires he was stifling, when, as far she was concerned, all he was succeeding in doing was releasing dormant passions within her.

She was determined to confront him and understand this paradox. The next weekend she went down to the cottage again. She stayed out of his sight Friday night and the greater part of the following morning. At about three o'clock on Saturday, when the sun was at its warmest, she went down to the boating dock. She knew he would have returned from his run and would be wrapping up his deep breathing by then. She had dieted all week and felt slimmer and more agile. She wore her black, two piece swim suit and did not take her wrap with her. She was going to be Iris at least for the next couple of hours. She even had Iris's book *The Black Prince* as a prop for the meeting.

"I looked up that word," she said, pulling a deck chair over and lying on it, her arms raised above her head.

He continued his deep breathing, looking away from her. Just when she was about to speak again to draw his attention, he said, "I'm glad you understand, now."

"I don't understand. It's selfish."

"Yet it's supposed to be the most self-less thing in the world. That's the eternal conundrum." He was towelling himself now and turning towards her, surveying her body on the deck chair.

"Is that why your wife left you?"

"I left her. It was the only way." Again, that sad look.

"It's too much to ask anyone. After all we are human," she said unapologetically.

He came over and hovered above her chair. The bulge in his shorts was at her eye level and she did not want to take her eyes off it.

He bent down to her, his breath inches from her face. She could smell the Indian spices emanating from his open, sweaty pores making him musky, mysterious.

"That is why I live alone now. I am practicing what we all should gravitate to in the end. But the rest of the world does not understand – does not let me be. My wife represented the rest of the world."

"And your children?"

"Yes, them too – they are my manifestations of desire. And that's why I don't write poetry – another desire."

"Why are you doing this?"

"It's my calling. At a certain point in their evolution, it's everyone's calling."

"Is that what you are putting in your book?"

"Yes. But it is a challenge for us mortals. I am on the cusp of either succeeding or failing."

She felt a stir of hope. He was not lost to asceticism yet. But who would have first claim to him if he turned back – his wife or Anne Jackson, widow and librarian?

As if in response he said, "My wife and I divorced two years ago when I chose Brahmacharya, before I came to the university. It was a formality, a barrier I needed to put between us, so that I would not to be pulled back."

He knelt by her this time and his breath was stronger on her face now. "But you are pulling me back. From the day I first laid eyes on you." She felt her nipples harden at his words. She wanted to grip him, pull him towards her, smother him with kisses and have him inside her, never to be released again.

She was reaching out, throwing all caution away – *Iris, you will be proud of me* –when he pulled back, stood up quickly and moved away. The spell was broken.

"Tomorrow – let it be tomorrow. Tonight I am writing the final chapter, my conclusion of this experiment. Tomorrow, I will know. Please wait until tomorrow." Then he hurried up the path leading to the annex and went indoors.

She flung *The Black Prince* deep into the lake and slumped back in the deck chair. "Iris – I bet you never had it this hard!" she shouted across the gently rolling waters.

*   *   *

She slept fitfully that night. Her body ached for him. She was aroused and hanging on the edge. "Damn him," she said for the umpteenth time as she rolled in bed, clamping a pillow firmly between her legs, determined not to give into those baser instincts that were trying to get out of control and spoil the purity she intended to share only with him.

She must have dozed around dawn, but woke when she heard an engine start nearby. Must be the garbage truck. She rolled back to sleep. Then woke with a start. She pulled on her housecoat hurriedly and ran barefoot to the back door. The lights were on in the annex.

"No, no!" She was shouting, running and panting up the steps of the annex to burst in through the front door, which, as usual, was unlocked.

The room was as clean as when she had leased it initially. All traces of Indian cooking had been scrubbed and Lysol'ed away. He was gone. On the desk was a manuscript with a note attached.

My dear Anne:

This manuscript is for you — it will never get published, for the hero never gets the girl in the end as he does in all good novels. But it helped me come to terms with myself. When I wrote the final chapter, I realized it is so easy to give up. But I have traveled too far and given up too much, to fail now. A marriage of twenty-five years, two accomplished children and a lifetime of learning, and hopefully, evolving. I have to continue my quest, as I am sure you have to continue yours. I am leaving early and do not expect a refund of the unused lease — in fact this manuscript is a gift to you for showing me the right path in my life – even though it may not coincide with yours. My best wishes to you – I am sure we will see each other at the university. I am sorry if I stirred emotions in you that were better left dormant. Perhaps, sometime in the future when our life passions have dried up, we will have the detachment to be friends. I asked this of my wife, but being many years younger than me, and the extraverted soul she is, she never understood.

Goodbye!

Ram

＊　＊　＊

That all happened five years ago. The manuscript was a story about a librarian and a professor who never consummated their feelings. She still works at the library and he has recently been awarded tenure at the university. He drops in to do his research from time to time, and they nod at each other and are civil. He looks calmer now, not so tormented. Over these five years she has had other sexual encounters but they have never had the wholeness that existed with Jack. And so she has compartmentalized her life with her late husband into a learning journey that began and ended, and does not need to be replicated. There is no more desperation to be joined with another in order to be whole. She *is* whole, and the detachment that she could not believe existed in humans, has begun to take hold.

She knocked down the annex and planted a few trees that now provide a new look and feel to the cottage property. She likes being alone now, and understands what the professor was pursuing. The other day, she wrote him a brief e-mail:

Dear Ram:

Sorry that it's taken five years to reply, but I was waiting for the detachment you described to arrive, before I could relate to you on your level. I think that I am almost there now. Would you like to take tea at the campus sometime and talk about that great subject of yours – desire?

When he responded, her heart pattered smoothly, free of the excitement of his earlier advances, and at ease with the finality of a milestone reached.

Dear Anne:

To say 'I like' would be desirous. Let's say that it would be 'mutually agreeable.' Three o'clock on Thursday afternoon? – Ram.

5

Turning Point

Harry Perkins adjusted his tie in the mirror and affirmed that the world was a good place that day. *Positive thinking, positive thinking.* Flecks of grey attacked his temples, and a fast-receding hairline threatened to bring a bald crown into view any day now. Despite the recent "casual dress" policy, he still wore a tie that captured the company's blue, enhanced by a red diagonal stripe. He put on the tweed jacket Marge had given him for Christmas five years ago and checked his briefcase. All the papers were there. He needed a lot of copies for his work. Harry placed his homemade sandwich – neatly wrapped in layers of plastic to prevent the mayonnaise from escaping – on top of the documents, and shut the case.

He examined himself once more. Experts said that men his age had to get rid of bifocals, but he was so used to his. Half-rimmed reading glasses were in vogue, not these ones that distorted one's features. He was diligent about trimming his eyebrows now, and those pesky nose and ear hairs. And he had to do something about the growing paunch, which his long treks to and from the subway and all that walking in the city did not control. *Think positive.*

He took a deep breath before his next action, willing himself to follow through. Exhaling, he called out loudly "Bye everybody – love you!" and went out the front door, hitting a stride for the next fifteen minutes that would take him to the subway by exactly 7:45 a.m.

At Kennedy Station, he took his usual seat facing the direction the train was heading; any other position made him dizzy. Over the top of his Globe & Mail, he surveyed the other passengers. The young woman in the blue suit (she never wore anything else – must be a uniform) had fallen asleep the moment the train left the station; probably exhausted with a demanding husband and young children keeping her awake at nights. School kids hung by the doors and yapped in loud expletives. He wondered if his Tania and Robert had done the same when they were that age; they had been such angels with mommy and daddy, but when they were with their friends …? He shuddered and shifted his gaze. Oh, no – the drunk was riding the rails again; sleeping on the train back and forth between Kennedy and Kipling. He'd probably hang in till noon, when renewed thirst would demand quenching. A $2.50 fare was a cheap substitute for the price of even the meanest flophouse. Harry looked out of the window, savouring the short outdoor run before the train plunged into the tunnel at Victoria Park. *No sense focusing on the losers!* Speaking of losers, he wondered whether the drunk had once been a privileged kid, given everything in life until one day the bottom fell out, leaving him with no resilience to pick up and go again; just ride the rails and drown out reality with booze. Harry shuddered again.

When he got off at King St., the swarm of office workers pushed him through the turnstiles. Blasts of cold spring air rushed down the entranceway steps. Cars honking in unforgiving traffic, and the bum on the sidewalk with a sign that read "Help me get home to the Maritimes," welcomed Harry to the rugged world he had survived the last thirty years. The city, unlike the suburbs, was magnetic, despite its ruthlessness. He could not imagine ever being away from it. He had tried to explain that to Marge, a freelance graphic designer unable to understand the nine-to-five life. There was a buzz here that he needed to propel his otherwise placid self into action. That was another reason he still came into the city every day, while Marge was following her own metamorphosis. Where would she be today? Must be Vancouver, on one of those designer tours that came as part of any new assignment she took.

Magnum Technologies occupied the top six floors of the new office tower at the corner of King and Yonge. Its huge neon commanded a formidable presence amidst the bank shingles that dominated the vicinity.

Harry felt his ears pop as he rode the express elevator to the twenty-eighth floor. He closed his eyes and took deep breaths to ward off dizziness. Muffled voices in the elevator spoke a different language these days.

"That system is state-of-the-art."

"What can I say – cutting edge technology and real-time delivery make us best-in-class."

"Certainly helps with the bottom line. Intellectual capital rules today."

"Elliott's a switched-on CEO. He turfed the process guys and brought in the knowledge workers. That's what's going to make him successful."

The voices exited on the twenty-sixth, the elevator's first stop and Magnum's new software division. Harry ascended the two remaining floors in peace.

Valerie greeted him with a smile as he came through the doors of the marketing department and went towards his corner nook. "Hi, Harry! How's the world today?"

"Pretty good. Pretty good." He looked forward to that greeting every morning. Val had been with the company as long as he had, and she always brought him his first coffee to get started. Her blonde hair was pulled back in a bun and she was wearing makeup today. It hid the rings around her eyes.

"The usual today?"

"Sure, Val." He smiled as he made his way over to his cubicle. Despite everything on her plate, she sure knew how to make his day.

He'd much preferred his old office, but with all the changes, he had to be "flexible." That was the new mantra. He retrieved the picture of Marge and the kids. The cleaners had knocked it off its stand again, and it lay buried under a pile of papers that had been moved. He had too many piles on his desk. Old Smiley, his former boss, had warned him about that. "Paper's going out; soft copies and e-mail are in; better get used to it." But Smiley had got canned in the first wave of re-structuring and Harry had stuck to his papers, even though their purpose had long expired. They kept him connected to his work.

He looked at the picture again; the stand needed fixing – he'd had it for too long. Marge looked much younger than she was today, but he liked to remember her like that – dark hair, outgoing features and a tilted nose that had once melted his heart. The children were pre-teens back then. He would play with them in the park, take Tania to dancing classes and Robert to hockey. He liked to freeze-frame them in that period, before adolescent angst, peer pressure and other distractions took control.

"They are so cute," Val said, handing him a steaming coffee mug.

Gratefully, he took it from her. "Yes they are, aren't they? Thanks, Val – you've been doing this for me all these years. You've always anticipated my every need …" He blushed and added, "in the office, that is."

"That's my job. Besides, you're worth it, Harry." For once, her chirpy countenance slipped and he saw the sadness in her eyes. In former times, Valerie had a cute habit of looking up in the air every time she said those words, a half-smile hiding somewhere in her wide mouth. But today she just looked tired.

"How's Bill?"

"Hanging on."

Bill, her husband, had been in and out of hospital with cancer for the last ten years.

"You are a loyal soul, Val. You stand by your man."

"What can I say, Harry; like you, I'm not a quitter."

*　*　*

"Just look at them rolling there, not a care in the world – like soulmates," Harry said. He was with Valerie in the park on their lunch break. College students were sitting on the grass; the serious ones had books spread out in front of them, others were locked, with varying intensity, in embrace. One couple had gone beyond the playful stage and was making out, blissfully unaware of the world. Their freedom made Harry envious.

"Sometimes, you just don't end up with the soulmate you look for," Valerie said, crumpling her sandwich bag and dusting the crumbs off her dress as she rose from the park bench. "Sorry I have to go. I've got to work through the rest of lunch." She was averting her eyes and he thought she was crying, in her silent way.

"What was that again? The soulmate bit?"

"Oh – something I've been reading recently. They say we go through life looking for a soulmate and some of us don't always find one in a particular incarnation."

"You've been reading New Age stuff?"

"I'm looking for something to believe in, Harry. I guess I need something to hang onto these days. I just wish it wasn't so. Now, I've really got to go. See you later."

He watched her hurry across the park.

Harry nibbled his sandwich. He always came out here at lunch time. Work/life balance; that was important. He wished he had pursued it much earlier in his career. Behind, the traffic roared. Ahead of him, the park and its lake with the swans calmed him. He ignored the frivolous young lovers and looked instead at the students who were reading their books on the grass. What did the parents of these studious ones do to keep them focused? He wished he knew.

Val joined him for lunch most days now and he was disappointed she had to cut out early today. He was spending a lot more "water cooler" time with her of late. She had been his administrative assistant once, the best he'd had, and Harry had always been proper throughout their working relationship. "Don't shit on your own doorstep", was the corporate mantra when it came to office dalliances, and Harry had followed that code to the letter. But now she worked for Walter, and her domestic circumstances made her want to talk more, and him to listen. Sometimes he talked too, while she listened.

His appointments across the city had been mixed this morning. Matheson's were looking to expand their business and would need what he had to offer shortly. "We'll call you," was how it ended, and that wasn't too promising. Harry had wished for a better closing. Saxon's Electronics was more favourable. They'd even talked "fees". Now, that was a sure buying signal. But Mr. Saxon was overseas, so the acting director couldn't make an instant decision but promised get back to him in a couple of weeks. The acting director seemed to look a bit crestfallen though, every time he glanced up. *Was it those damn bifocals?*

Walking back to his desk, Harry peeked into his old office. Walter was back, hands behind his head, leaning in the chair with his legs up on the table. He must have just returned from another liquid lunch with the ad agency. "Yeah, let's price them at fifty percent for this promo – Elliott won't mind – this is software. The marginal cost is that of a CD and packaging."

Harry grunted as he overheard Walter's deal-making. *These MBA types - they cut deals to make short term profits that screwed up long term cash flow.*

Harry's afternoon went briskly – many calls to be made to new prospects. He even managed to get two more face-to-face meetings arranged. These days he dwas getting better at it; his call-to-appointment ratio had improved from fifty-to-one to about fifteen-to-one. This is what excited him, even in his present circumstances – the frenetic activity over the phone, the negotiating, the wins and losses – the excitement of not knowing how the next transaction would turn out. Ever since he had been a young marketing apprentice back in the seventies, office buzz had intoxicated him like a jolt of java, and it pre-occupied him until the janitor wheeling his cart down the corridors had to remind him it was well past closing time, or Marge called to say that Robert had got yet another note from school for not doing his homework, and when was Harry thinking of addressing the issue? A light cough disturbed his thoughts.

"How's the relocation project going, Harry?"

Elliott Magnum, thirty five, and now President and CEO of Magnum Industries was surveying him from that neutral space just outside his cubicle. Elliott was short like his father, but Magnum Sr. had been kind. With his casual dress, golf shirt and khaki slacks, Elliott could have just been returning from the eighteenth hole at Angus Glen, and he probably was. Harry realized that this must be Elliott's day for "walking among the troops," otherwise the CEO never descended from his executive suite on the thirty second floor. Elliott was tossing his ever present squeeze ball from hand to hand – he was known to run through dozens of these stress relievers a month, especially in the heat of meetings when he threw them at subordinates.

Harry bit his lip. It was hard to take Elliott seriously, let alone show him respect. After all, he was the summer student who had come to Harry to learn how to create a sales promotion kit not that many years ago. Harry realized, even back then, that his protégé was not very bright. What was he to do with this kid who had mixed up the logos going down to the print shop? Costly rework and delay in production had resulted. But you never fired the chairman's son, or even reprimanded him. Harry however, had given Elliott firm feedback on being prepared and having a method to one's madness. The apprentice had glared back, then walked away smiling. He did not re-appear until Magnum Sr. retired last year. In the intervening years, Elliott had built a resume of business success in the US and Europe that no one could verify. Now at the helm, Elliott was determined to change the face of Magnum and its employees forever.

Be upbeat and don't show him your true feelings, Harry reminded himself. In fact, that was yet another corporate mantra – "never show them when you're down, or it gets worse."

"It's going well. I should wrap up this project inside the month," he said.

"Good. I can't hold out any longer. We have to get on with our plans too."

Which don't include real people, you young bastard! If your Dad hadn't intervened, you would have carried on regardless. Harry shoved the thought away and smiled. "Well, I'd better get back to my calls. I want to snag one more appointment before closing time."

"You're a good man, Harry," Elliott maintained his toothy grin, but when his squeeze ball changed hands again, it looked like a flattened turd. The CEO quickly skipped over to the next cubicle. Harry's enthusiasm evaporated with Elliott's departure.

Valerie came by at 3:15.

"Want to go for a coffee?" Harry asked eagerly. Then he realized this was not going to happen; she had her jacket and bag in hand.

"I can't today. Got to take Bill down to the hospital for his test results. That's why I worked through lunch, so Walter wouldn't gripe."

"Is Bill all right? You never said anything at lunch."

"We'll know when we get the results – no sense in panicking anyone. He hasn't been doing too grand lately, though."

"Shall I phone you later this evening to find out?"

She raised her eyebrows, but not in defence – this was the first time he had offered to call her at home since she stopped reporting to him, and even when he had called in the past, it was always business related. "Not sure when I will be home. But try about nine. I'll probably need to talk to someone by then. Bye Harry."

"Take it easy, Val. I'll call you." *What the heck am I doing? Stepping out of the comfort zone? But it sure feels good!*

He took his coffee break alone. Amidst the clatter of the downstairs cafeteria he was alone in his thoughts as he sat by the window and watched the traffic go by. The bum was still begging outside the subway entrance, now with a couple of companions; they were having smokes and coffee as they went about their "work". None of them seemed in a hurry to get back to the Maritimes or wherever.

Harry stirred his coffee aimlessly. He did not want to drink it anymore. Something was building inside him, like a dam about to burst, something over which he had no control.

At four-thirty, back at his desk, with the last five calls leading to dead ends, Harry reached a conclusion. "I CAN'T KEEP UP THIS FAÇADE ANYMORE!" The dam had burst. A nervous administrative assistant in the vicinity, jumped, averted her eyes, and hurried away. He packed up his things, looked at the family photograph one more time, and dumped it into his briefcase too. A feeling of lightness coursed though him as he made his way to the exit.

"Going home, already?" Walter called from his office.

"Yes. I suddenly realized that I am not a slave anymore, like you and everyone else in this place." Harry loosened his tie.

Walter swallowed. "Hey, hey – why so touchy, all of a sudden?"

"I'm free Walter, and it takes a while getting used to it. I may not even come in tomorrow. And Elliott can't do a thing about it. Try that for one, if you dare."

He left Walter grasping for a retort, and headed for the doors. He pitched his tie into the waste bin in the corridor before stepping inside the elevator. Oh, that felt so good!

The trip home was the hardest part for him these days. Today was no exception as his elation over telling Walter off evaporated. At the subway station, he leaned his back against the wall, scared of the strange feeling that overcame him every time he stood near the edge of the platform. Today that urge was really strong, so he moved away from the wall and sat down on a bench right in the middle, between the east and west-bound platforms, and closed his eyes until his train arrived, and the familiar chimes announced that the doors had opened. Then he darted into the carriage directly in front of him and squeezed in just as the chimes rang again.

Rush hour, with its tired, moody and less-forgiving multitudes, had already begun. The air was saturated with body odour. No one gave the very pregnant woman in the aisle a seat, and Harry himself standing, couldn't help. A man elbowed his way to the doors at Castle Frank, and nearly knocked the woman down. "Fucker!" she shouted back at him. Harry closed his eyes and prayed for the ride to end soon.

Disembarking at Kennedy, he walked home slowly. He was surprised there was still daylight; he normally came home in darkness. The mornings were so much better. The city, despite its energy, sapped him throughout the day; the frenetic human activity that boiled within it, its myriad ambitions, actions, neuroses and prejudices, drained as much as it energized. It was like taking alcohol or drugs – the rapid high then the slow descent.

The silence of the house was less frightening now, but still depressing. He skipped the customary, "I'm home!" It was not like in the days when the photograph in the office was taken, when there had always been the laughter of children and the smell of cooking to welcome him home. He switched on the lights as he made his way into the kitchen. The answering machine was flashing. He dropped the mail on the kitchen table. He was afraid to listen to the voice messages. They were usually calls of rejection, and he could only take so many of those in a day. They had started with the one from Marge, telling him she was going to live with her mother because he was married to his job, and she had stopped growing in the marriage.

He went through the mail instead. The usual bills he laid aside. The letters from the Mason and Fitch Employment Agency he did not want to open – they phoned if they struck gold; they wrote in all other instances. The letter he had been expecting any day now from Marge's lawyer had finally arrived. Yes, yes, he knew – so he had not met the alimony payments for the last three months. And he would like to see how far her jaw would drop when he wrote to tell her why. There was one from Robert's parole officer; the boy had not been keeping his appointments again. Robert, growing up well provided for and spoiled; drugs had been an easy out for him. Now he lived in some hovel downtown with a bunch of like-minded losers. Harry had not seen his son in months. *Where did I let him down?*

By giving him too much? Maybe Robert was addicted to drugs just like Harry was addicted to the city. *Each to his own!*

He pressed the switch of the answering machine with a sigh. Thankfully, there was only one message today.

"Dad – Hi! How's work? Um, I need some money. Could you manage two hundred? These tuition fees are killing me. And my library job is also ending in the summer. Call me – Love you! Bye."

The little girl in his picture had grown up. But Tania was still his little girl, she still needed him. His eyes swelled with tears of pride. She was the only one who called these days, even if it was just for money. And she was at least trying – like him. Even though he still paid her insurance and the loan on the car he had bought for her eighteenth birthday.

He got up and put the kettle on; he had stopped drinking alcohol, afraid of where in his present circumstances, one drink could lead. So he drank tea instead. He took out a pack of Swanson's from the freezer and popped it into the microwave. He would need to replenish his stock of frozen dinners this weekend.

He went over to the hall mirror and re-appraised his "product" again.

"Remember, *you* are your product." The outplacement counsellor had drilled it into them. "You are selling *you.*"

If not for old Mr. Magnum, Harry's severance package would have been much smaller, and Elliott would not have given him the corner cubicle to work on his "relocation" over the past three months. And there was only one month left before that lifeline too, ended. Elliott's form of rationalizing had been more like rape. He hated the people with experience because they made him feel inadequate. So he got rid of them and Harry had been foremost in the new CEO's sights.

He looked in the mirror again. *Screw the relocation project and the deadline to find another job! Even the bums in this country make a living, and nobody starves. Time to do things in style and damn the clock. Time to be Harry Perkins, whoever that guy is.* Yes, he would go for a bit of a nip and tuck with the rest of his severance. And dye his hair black. And maybe, if his finances permitted, join a gym and do something about that paunch. And the bi-focals would definitely have to go. Why not lop ten years from his resume as well – resumes lied, anyway. "Product enhancement" they called it in marketing lingo. He'd done it with all the products he had marketed at Magnum over the years – why not with himself? It was time to re-launch the new and improved Harry Perkins!

And he would finally write that letter to Marge, telling her that he had lost his job. He'd let Tania know too when he called her back this time. He wondered if his daughter would stop calling after that, or call more often when her debts started catching up with her. It would be a good test of her real feelings towards Dad. Robert wouldn't care; he'd be too stoned to even remember.

Harry had been ducking this decision – after all, his job had defined him. It was what Marge had come to expect from him at a minimum when the children had left the nest and sex and companionship became stale. And love? That too wanes when needs remain unfulfilled. It was easier to admit that his hair was thinning than to admit not having a job. He'd never been without one. And that's why he kept toiling away after everyone in his family had left – to earn their love by at least meeting their financial needs. Marge had gambled on that, for sure, so her financial pipeline could be secure while she explored new opportunities.

He set the microwave to cook for five minutes and made his tea. Just then the phone rang.

"Hi Harry? Thank God it's you!"

"Val. You're home already?" He was surprised too – this was the first time she had called him at home since she had stopped being his assistant.

"No, I'm in the hospital. They've found something on Bill again – this time it's terminal. Oh, Harry ..."

He wanted to put his arms around her and comfort her, just like he had comforted Marge when they had faced so many family trials in the past. But Marge had stopped playing on his team and left to develop her own talents; now his arms reached into empty space.

"I'll be with you Val. Don't worry."

"You've got your own problems Harry."

"Problems are best shared. Not in an empty house where I am now. That's where you will be, when Bill is gone."

"I'm sorry to bother you like this Harry."

"It's okay – I'm happy you called. This has been the best call of my day."

"What do you mean?"

"Never mind. Are you staying at the hospital tonight?"

"I guess so."

"I could bring some food over. And we can keep vigil together."

"But you have work tomorrow. I mean - you have work to do tomorrow."

"I have worked enough. Besides, I don't think I'm going in

tomorrow. I want to do things at my pace for a while. Relate to the people who care for me instead. And I am going to upgrade my product too. I'll explain when I come over." He cradled the portable phone, shut off the microwave and pitched the Swanson's package into the trash.

"I'm not sure what's got into you Harry, but I can certainly do with some company."

He was whistling now, the letters from the employment agency landed in the trash right on top of the half-cooked dinner. "I'm coming. And you can tell me all about soulmates to take your mind off things."

"You're a good man, Harry."

6

Rage

Nelly sat at the window and watched the sunset creep across a dark, cloud-streaked sky. Soon Jeb would be home with the candy. She'd reminded him the whole week and he had grunted when he left this morning. She needed the candy. The children avoided her doorstep like the plague, called her the wicked witch and Jeb a pervert – except on Halloween night, when candy melted their prejudices.

Nelly touched the children, brushing her fingers along their outstretched arms as she handed out the sweets. The touch of children was full of life and so unlike touching the stuffed animals that stood in all corners of the house, handiwork from her stint at the taxidermist. She'd never been touched the way she had wanted to be touched – by caring parents, by a lover, a friend, by offspring – she had none, never known any either. Oh, Jeb touched her all right; but that was not how she wanted it – not with his rancid, nicotine tinged, raspy breath, and that bulge rising around his crotch that he kept rubbing with one hand as he touched her down *there* with his other. No, that was not what she wanted. When she touched the children, they innocently looked into her eyes and reciprocated in a way that was so rewarding. They did not notice the gnarled fingers that had long ago lost their gentleness from too many chemicals in her bloodstream.

Yes, this was her day – Halloween – when she would feel the contact of other human beings and she looked forward to it so much. Especially after the fall last year that had stolen her mobility. No more going to the mall, pinching Jeb's car, even though she didn't have a driver's license, and scooting off when he was asleep; no more watching people go by in the park. Now she was bound to this house, the wheelchair and this steel cane with its big handle that Jeb insisted she have in case of another "accident".

Fancy leaving oil on the steps to the basement – he was so careless. Or was he? She had run down to get her laundry and that was her last-ever trip to the basement. She wriggled her lifeless legs and thought they moved a bit. Progress? Next year, it will be better, she reminded herself.

For the last ten years they had lived together; but she did not like Jeb, even though he was her brother and only living relative. He had bullied her ever since she was five, and he was ten. That was in their first foster home. There may have been other times before, but all she could recall were angry faces, raised voices and being spanked even when she was watching TV and staying out of trouble. But at five she remembered Jeb telling her that she was going to be his slave and he was the sultan. He'd dress himself up with old clothes and tell her to show her breasts to him – she had none at five, so she took off her tee shirt and followed him around in her panties. And he would pull her by the hair and bonk her on the head for no reason. After a while, she just endured it – it was easier, though painful. If Jeb felt in control, she knew he would protect her from other neighbourhood bullies.

Then they took Jeb away. He had been suspected of lighting fires near the Dawson's shed, and one day the gas barbecue exploded. The soot all over his face gave the game away. That was the first day she saw him cry. He had wanted his sister, but she was not allowed to go with him.

A few years later, her foster father, a dirty drunkard, forced his way on her. If Jeb had been around it would never have happened. She was bloody and dirty and sore for days. Then he came to her room almost nightly while his pregnant wife lay ill in bed. Before she knew it, things started to happen in her own belly, and she was sick every morning. When they aborted the baby, she cried. They said since she was a "simple" kid, and could be getting into further "trouble", she must undergo an operation to fix things permanently. And she cried again when that happened.

Afterwards she was sent to a convent. "Need to bring you up, good and proper and save your miserable soul," Sister Phyllis would say. Sister Phyllis, or "Syphilis" as the other girls would whisper, was a tyrannical, long-nosed woman in her mid forties. If you did not have your bed made by six a.m., there was punishment; dishes not cleaned after meals and there was more punishment; homework not done – greater punishment. Punishment came in the form of a cane applied smartly on the backside. On the numerous occasions it was meted out to Nelly, she always heard the close, heavy breathing of the grim, purposeful nun.

She started to have blackouts around that time, followed by periods when she would steal away into the woods nearby and beat her hand against a tree until it was raw and the pain in her head cleared. The more she hit the tree, the better she felt, becoming oblivious to the damage to her own body. When the scars on her hands were discovered, there was more punishment, but she no longer cried.

She got into real trouble the day Sister Phyllis put her to work at dawn cleaning the yard. It was a frosty fall day with leaves scattered everywhere. She had to fill six bags before breakfast. "Syphilis" interrupted her when she had stuffed her fifth, and said they weren't filled enough, so she had to untie and top them up again. When she had placed the bursting sixth bag in the shed and got to the dining hall, breakfast was over. She had to content herself with leftovers in the kitchen. Then it was washing up duty as one of the girls had called in sick. She was late for Sister Martha's English class, and her homework was incomplete.

"Detention today, Sister?" she moaned. "It's movie day." She was looking so forward to seeing Mary Poppins.

"You will do as you are told, young lady."

She missed the movie and ended up completing her homework in the library. As she was fantasizing about going to the woods and beating a tree again, she felt a painful tug. Sister Phyllis was wringing her ear.

"You silly girl! The bags were too tight. They burst going into the garbage truck. The leaves are all over the backyard again and it's another whole week until the truck returns. Get out there right now and redo those bags."

"But my homework –..."

"I don't care about your homework!"

A smack on the side of her head emphasized the point. Maybe it was the smack that did it. Lights, red and hazy, blurred

Nelly's vision and her head hummed. Sister Phyllis loomed in front of her like a big tree - a tree that needed to be beaten so that her pain would ease. So Nellie beat the tree – repeatedly. At first the tree looked surprised and refused to yield. Then it wailed, wilted and collapsed, motionless on the floor. And Nelly felt better.

They put her in a mental home and on drugs that made her sick and woozy. She hardly knew if it was night or day, nor did she care. All she could remember were the odd, unexpected screams from her fellow inmates and the stern nurses who came by with those infernal medications. But that was also where she met Hazel who became her only companion – the rest preferring to talk to themselves, even laughing at their own jokes.

Hazel was ninety and suffering from Alzheimer's. When she was coherent, Hazel would tell stories about her life as an orphan, how she landed in Canada as a war bride, had three children and lost them all in a house fire, lost her husband to cancer, lost her life savings to a loan shark and ended up in this home when she had become a bit "overwhelmed". Sometimes her stories had different endings but Hazel was always optimistic. Despite her failing memory, she planned to be out by next year, and always bolstered Nelly's spirits by saying, "Now remember child, next year it will be better."

The following summer, when Nelly was transferred to work in a hospice, Jeb tracked her down and visited. He was a grown man now and had put on a lot of weight. He was accompanied by a shy, retiring young woman whom he introduced as Alice, his wife.

"Where've you been all these years, Jebby?"

"I made it Nelly! They couldn't put me down!" He went on

to say that he was a real estate salesman and had done some big deals. "You could come live with us, Nelly."

But she was still serving a suspended sentence for manslaughter and had to remain under supervision at the hospice. Jeb and Alice visited her frequently after that. On every occasion Jeb's affluence was increasing – he showed off the car he had purchased and pictures of the new house in Brampton.

"Now you can have a baby!" Nelly said.

Alice pulled a face.

Then their visits stopped abruptly. Nelly tried to contact them from the payphone in the hospice but there was no answer. Three months later, a pale, worn-looking Alice came alone to visit.

"I'm moving back to Nova Scotia. Came to say goodbye. Jeb's in prison."

The real-estate stuff had been a big scam. The market had collapsed and Jeb had gone down under a mountain of debt, losing clients' monies he'd been rolling with.

Nelly wished she could cry. She couldn't even feel rage anymore because of the medication. "And you two didn't even have time to have the baby!" she said.

Alice winced. "Baby – fat chance – your brother can't have any babies. We tried. His sperm's dead."

She never saw Alice again. Nelly served out her ten-year sentence in the hospice, helping people die with dignity. But she was still sentenced to a life of taking drugs that would balance her "urges". Upon her release, she visited the mental home to see Hazel again, only to learn that the old lady had died two months after her departure. Hazel had got her wish all right – "next year" had brought her release, and maybe a casket had been the "better" thing.

The only work Nelly could get after that was with the taxidermist. She learned a new trade stuffing dead animals, and kept some of them in the only dwelling she could afford – a shack by the railway tracks. She had a stuffed parrot, a cat, a raccoon and a squirrel. But she longed for real living things. That was why she loved watching the children in the playground. But their mothers seemed to have warned them off; every time she tried inviting the children over to her humble abode, they refused to come. They called her the 'bag lady".

Then Jeb showed up again – thinner, greyer, he'd lost two front teeth and looked at her strangely. "I'm going to teach those bastards," was all he said repeatedly on that first visit. He visited regularly after that and appeared to be getting back rapidly into the stream of life following his incarceration.

"I'm a distributor," he said one day. She did not understand. "For a photographer," was all the explanation he gave.

Then he asked her to move in with him. "You're living in this little shack," he said. "I've got a bungalow with a garden and you can have a room to yourself."

"And you won't play 'slave' with me?" she asked.

He laughed. "Oh no, Nelly. If you just cook for me – that would be fine."

So she left her job and moved in with him and took the stuffed animals with her. At first, life was fine. Jeb did not have any visitors and did not encourage her to have any either. There was a big garden out back of the house – Jeb had neglected it and she cleaned it up and planted flowers like she had been taught in the convent. Soon she was spending all her time in the garden. The plants were her children.

Jeb had a computer and an office in the basement. He spent

hours there. He would print things and put them in a fat envelope and go away for awhile. She had never seen a computer, having missed most of the last thirty years of what had gone on in the world. At first she was afraid to go near it.

But she was intrigued by his car – she'd always wanted to drive one. And one day she did, when he was fast asleep after one of his nights out. He had about two or three of those nights every week. She knew he was going out when he took one of those blue pills. But the car had been fun even though many other drivers had honked at her. She was obviously breaking all the rules, but it gave her the freedom she'd never had before. As long as a cop did not pull her over, and as long as she could get back before Jeb woke up, she was safe. As for her driving skills, she kept saying to herself, "Next year, it will be better."

The lift in her spirits with the garden and the car made her stop taking her medication. She felt she did not need it anymore. She did not tell Jeb about it, or he would be mad. And she started to feel better, clearer. But it also made her more aware of Jeb's visits to her room at night to touch her. That was on the nights he did not go out. He would not say anything and she would keep her eyes closed and pretend she was asleep. She did not like the way he touched her. Later they never talked about it. But she felt as if this was yet another obligation she owed him for not having to play "slave".

Things went wrong again the day Mrs. Hawk's big Alsatian peed on her roses. She was in the garden shearing the hedge, when the animal came through the break in the fence that she'd been meaning to mend, sniffed around the rose bush, brazenly lifted its leg and sent a stream of hot urine into the plant. Those lights that had been absent all the years she had been on medication started going wild in her head again, and before she knew what, she had driven the clippers through the dog's neck. It did not take long to die. When her head cleared, she took the cadaver indoors and hid it in the basement, thinking she'd stuff it later. She prayed that Mrs. Hawk would never find out. But Jeb came home and blew his top. He checked her medication and knew she'd been cheating. He took the carcass out that night and buried it in the back yard. From then on, he supervised her closely. He also hid the car keys, having become suspicious of her wanderings. She did not much care to go into the backyard after that, because she imagined the decaying remains of that horrid animal oozing out and poisoning her "children". The flowers withered and died soon after.

One day when Jeb was out, her search for the spare car keys led to his office. The computer was on. Tentatively, she tapped on the silent keyboard and the dark screen came to life with pictures of young girls – lots of them. Beautiful, naked pre-teens. Some had older men touching them and doing things to them – like Jeb did to her at night. Disgusted and scared, she ran back upstairs.

That was when she thought of leaving and going back to her shack.

"And how are you going to manage on your ownsome?" he said sarcastically.

"I can work at the taxidermist again."

"And what if I tell about Mrs. Hawk's dog?"

"And what are you doing with all those young girls' pictures?" she countered.

"I told you – I'm a distributor. It's art. You're not educated enough to understand," he said smugly.

"But they're children."

"They are little pests." Jeb had never liked children. That's why he couldn't have any, she thought.

Then he tried placating her. He showed her his bank balance and said there was enough money for both of them – that he would be leaving her everything if he passed away prematurely. Wouldn't she stay?

But she still wanted to leave. She packed her things in stages and whenever he was out of the house, she took bits away and stowed them in the luggage office at the railway station. But she should not have touched her stuffed animals. For one day he asked her out of the blue, "Where's the parrot and the racoon?"

"I got rid of them. Don't like them anymore," she said, looking down at the floor, all the while thinking of those two stuffed animals reposing in their plastic covers in the luggage office.

He stayed home more often, but then at nights his demands on her body became more desperate. She was reaching her limit, so one morning she announced, "I'm leaving!"

That evening she went in the basement to get her clothes from the dryer and pack her suitcase and slipped on the greased stairs. She was never able to leave the house on her own again.

The sound of Jeb's car broke her troubled reminiscence. He'd be bringing the candy and the children would be coming soon and that was just what she needed today, to forget the past – even for a little while. Over the last couple of weeks, she had also found a way to stop her medication again without Jeb finding out. She needed the heightened sensation of those children's touches and the medication usually deadened all that. Now when Jeb gave her the pill each morning, she put it in her mouth, lodged it between tongue and tooth and gulped her water quickly. Then when he had turned his back she took it out and hid it in her dressing gown to flush down the toilet later. Thus she was feeling clear-headed and excited today.

"Did you bring the candy?" she asked eagerly, turning away from the window. He was coming in through the door, carrying grocery bags.

"No."

"What do you mean – no?"

"That's what I said – no. You're wasting money on those pesky creatures."

"But you promised …!"

"Never mind that I promised. You shouldn't have them coming up to the house. It could ruin my business."

"But Jebby …it's Halloween. It's the only day."

"Listen. I'm the breadwinner here, okay? What I say goes. I don't want any kids messing around here." He went off into the kitchen with the grocery bags and she heard the familiar pop of a beer can opening.

She turned towards the window, her eyes brimming with tears, surprised she could cry again. Maybe it was because the medication had worn off. The streetlights had come on and the first few prowlers were out, dressed in natty witch and goblin costumes. One caped figure with a basket popped onto her porch. Its little lips formed the familiar "trick or treat?"

Nelly was shaking. If only she had the candy, she would have been reaching out to those tiny arms, holding them, stroking them and placing the treats in them. She did not want to open the window and tell the creature to come back, perhaps tomorrow, when she would have time to call Wheel-Trans and go down to the store to get the sweet stuff. Because children never returned the following day. Only next year at this time. A whole year to wait.

Then the little creature, having waited too long for a door that didn't open, took out what looked like an egg and dashed it on the porch and turned on its heel.

"No… wait!" Nelly had the window open by now and was calling after the child, who was fast disappearing into the gloom. But all she heard floating back to her was, "… the bag lady is a witch!"

She slumped in her chair. Those bright lights and buzzing sounds were in her head again. "Oh, no… not now, dear God!"

"Here's your dinner." Jeb approached, a plate in one hand, a glass of water in the other and a smile on his face. The master was feeding his slave and feeling in control.

That's when she hit him with the metal walking stick. Right in the middle of his forehead. He looked confused, even amused for a moment, until the plate and glass fell out of his hands. She hit him again and again and again. Once for the orphanages, another for the cruel sisters, once each for every opportunity denied her in life and there were many hits to record. Jeb was a mighty big tree and took all her blows.

When her head had cleared, Jeb was sprawled in front of her, his battered face a mass of blood.

"If you'd only bought the candy," she sighed. A surge of freedom coursed through her. All restrictions were gone, except for the wheelchair. Each blow she struck had released and paid off every past injustice. Now she could throw away those awful medications because there was no one left to harm or stifle her. And she would mold Jeb. She could imagine his stuffed carcass filling the space left by the parrot and raccoon. And she would reshape his face to look handsome, not the toothless wretch he had become.

She heard the sound of more "trick or treaters" coming down the lane and quickly shut the window and switched off the porch light. She needed to lie down.

As she drew away from the window, she waved at the dim forms of vampires and fairies outside. "Goodnight dearies; see you next Halloween. And next year, it will be better – I promise."

7

Unattainable

Beatrice is at her customary perch by the bay window of the living room. The winter sun streams in and the snow has turned into gleaming ice. She is glad that the grocer delivered her provisions for the coming week. This is horrible weather to go out in. She knows Hercules will nevertheless be taking his daily constitutional around this time and it is an event she does not want to miss. She hopes "the muddles" will not bother her today.

On the stained coffee table by her side, the papers she has just signed glare back at her, but she does not want to look at them again. *Signing one's life away – that's what it amounts to.* She is wry-faced. *But how can I manage this house any more?* She has lived here thirty years. Single women did not buy houses and live on their own in those days; they got married, but Beatrice was the exception. As one of the early women PhD's that went onto tenured faculty positions at the university, she had her life and income mapped out for her. She was independent, and still is… except for these papers…

There are times now when her mind wanders. The doctors had warily used the dreaded "A" word, albeit early onset symptoms of it. "My foot!" she thunders in the confines of her home. "I had… have… one of the most brilliant minds," and to remind herself and shut out her mounting fear, she lays out faded press clippings on the coffee table that showcased her once stellar academic career.

She takes a sip from her cup of tea, steam rising in the sun rays that flow in through the window, and pushes her head into the wingback chair. Memories come flooding in. Perhaps it's these memories that get in the way and make her forget where she is, and allow the doctors to say she suffers from dementia.

Her thoughts take her back to the week she moved into this suburban neighbourhood. Her books took up most of the packing cases. The new furniture, ordered from Simpson's, had still to arrive. No one had offered to help her move – the men at the university called her frigid and standoffish; the women were jealous of her academic credentials.

As she hauled the heavy boxes, perspiration, prompted by exertion and the stifling summer heat, broke out all over her body. One of the boxes caught on the screen door and fell from her hand, spewing heavy hard-covers down the steps and onto the driveway.

Just then, a pick-up stopped at the curb and the driver stuck his head out. Curly, long black hair and muscular bare arms were all she could see.

"Need-a some help, miss?"

The label "Hercules the Handyman" on the vehicle drew a haughty defensive laugh from her, which helped hide her embarrassment about being so clumsy. She straightened up, patting back her hair, conscious of the dark stains spreading under her arms onto her indigo-blue blouse.

"How much do you charge?" she shot back.

The man got out of the truck. He wore faded khaki overalls and a sleeveless white undershirt. He was chunky and broad-shouldered, just under six feet in height. When he smiled he showed milky-white teeth, perfectly set. His eyes were black diamonds, accentuated by a few days' stubble. An oval medal and crucifix hung from a gold chain around his neck and embedded themselves in thick matted chest hair.

"It's no problem," he said, and began picking up the books.

When he passed her and made his way to enter the house, she smelled his manly odour, and a hint of tobacco. She caught her breath. *He's just an ignorant worker. But he's so unlike the namby-pamby types in the university. He's so... so real!*

"I insist on paying," she said following him into the house, unable to stop him from doing the job he assumed was his.

He surveyed the boxes of books inside, scratching his head. "This all-a you got?"

She blushed. "The rest of my stuff is coming shortly."

"You don't go lifting all-a this stuff, okay, miss? I gonna help you."

"How much do you charge?"

He ignored her again and started moving the boxes from various places she had dropped them to a central area in the empty hall.

"Miss – you read-a the books, I arrange them, okay?"

He fished a card from his back pocket. Their hands touched as he placed the card in hers; his fingers were rough and hard, but they transferred confidence and strength, affirming the fledgling belief that this move was not a mistake.

"I do this for you for free today, okay? When the rest of your stuff comes, I charge you $15.00 per hour – half my regular price, okay?"

"Do you do electrical too?"

"Electrical, plumbing, carpenting. I am handyman. Even take-a care of your car for you."

After the last box was in place, he grinned and strode past her to his truck. Again the whiff of manliness that made her weak as their bodies grazed in the doorway.

*   *   *

She stirs in the chair. Had she fallen asleep? Has he gone past the house already? For a moment she panics. Then she settles back in her chair. It hasn't gone past ten yet. He always goes by a few minutes after ten.

Her mind drifts again.

Hercules fixed her place "up-a good," as he would have said. When her precious family heirlooms arrived out of storage the following day – the Steinway piano handed down the generations in her family, her late parents' double bed and wardrobe closet bequeathed to her – he came out to help again. He was reluctant to enter her bedroom, and finally agreed to haul the bed and closet with an assistant he had hired only for that purpose.

He also helped move the furniture ordered from Simpson's, which the deliveryman had piled in her driveway, as she discovered, upon arriving home from work a few evenings later.

"These-a big department stores – only take-a your money -

charging too much for plywood at bottom with veneer on the top. I make-a better for you," he said, pronouncing judgment when the furniture was in place.

Under her commission, Hercules ripped out the old wiring and replaced the fuse box with one conforming to the new provincial electrical code. He built additional shelves in the kitchen and down in the basement. When he offered to make her a dining room suite - the only furniture missing to complete the house she declined, preferring to order one from Eaton's that she had been eyeing for its traditional style and five-year warranty. He retreated outdoors and repaired the weathered fence and painted it a bright red.

The following summer he built her a shed. It took two months, as he did the work in his spare time. She loved to watch him work, stealing glimpses of his muscles, the thick tufts of hair under his arms, the strong legs. She even tolerated his breaks when he smoked a cigarette with a far off look on his face. Whenever he looked her way, she pretended to be busy. She played her piano and deliberately lapsed into Italian favourites at times, if only to hear his belting tenor rendering "O Solo Mio" with gusto. Yet her heart was heavy, for she knew that she could only look. Too much distance existed between them to do any more.

After the garden shed was complete, Hercules announced, "Miss Betty – you must come to my house for barbecue. Next Saturday, my oldest daughter's tenth birthday. You must meet-a my wife and my bambini. Also my mother."

Beatrice accepted the invitation and went up the street to the Olivettis with some trepidation. Instead of seeing a big Italian family, she was surprised to see most of the neighbourhood gathered in the backyard. She felt guilty; she had lived on this street for over a year and had made no friends or invited anyone over. Between excited children running about and adult neighbours chatting in little groups, she caught sight of Hercules manning a steaming barbecue, heaving out sausages, steaks, kebabs, burgers and potatoes to a short woman at his side who was serving them to the guests. When the woman approached her with a plate of steaming sausages and potato wedges, Beatrice studied her closely. The woman wore her coarse black hair in an untidy bouffant, her features were plain, with a hint of moustache that gave her a bossy air; she was dressed in a faded green dress that was too long and too tight; her hips bulged and her calves protruded like hams.

"Hello, I am Beatrice – Betty," She wanted to be friendly. The woman scrutinized her, holding on to the plate of food reluctantly.

"The professor lady?" There was a trace of envy in the sunken eyes; the nose sniffed like a bitch surveying suspicious new food. She stuck the tray out at Beatrice. "Here – you want?"

"No thank you. I'll just have a drink."

The woman shouted at a shy retiring girl of about eight who was balancing a tray of soft drinks in her hands and looking overworked. "Giovanna, get the Coke to this lady." Then the woman nodded and hurried past to a clump of guests.

Drink in hand, Beatrice wandered around the large backyard. Discount-store garden gnomes littered the yard. She thought smugly about the two she had bought at an expensive antique sale in Port Hope last summer. She went indoors in search of a washroom. The house was deserted. The kitchen was a mess of raw meat in various stages of preparation for the barbecue, with flies flitting in, despite the screen door, to keep guard and nibble. Opened bottles of pop stood around losing their fizz, and a bag of buns had burst, its contents fallen on the floor. Beatrice edged into the tight guest washroom that shocked her senses with its bright yellow walls and dark purple curtains; however the plumbing worked very efficiently and there was plenty of toilet paper – rolls of it stacked on the floor. Afterwards, she stole through the hall for a further glimpse into the lives of the Olivettis. The passageway was crammed with children's bicycles, skates hanging on the walls, tennis rackets and a jumble of shoes. The living room walls were painted in sky blue and indigo framing huge farm-scene murals. A television set blared with no audience; still more shoes lay scattered about, and a treadle sewing machine sat off to the side, supporting a pile of cloth cuttings. The dining table was hand-made of tough, unpolished oak. Beatrice was glad she had bought hers from Eaton's.

Something was missing and she scanned the room once more, and sure enough, in an alcove, a red oil lamp burned, highlighting pictures of the Madonna and Child, framed inside a little grotto nailed to the wall. As Beatrice stepped out, she couldn't help but feel the vibrancy of life emanating from that jumble of possessions, reflecting the personalities of the family that lived in this house. Her home was so sterile in comparison.

Outdoors once more, Beatrice sidled over to where Hercules was flipping burgers and holding forth with a couple of guests.

"Ah, Miss Betty – you have come." Hercules' smile was wide and his demeanour brightened upon seeing her.

You have met-a my wife – Anna?" he gestured towards the busy serving woman, and Beatrice nodded.

"… And my mamma?"

"Your mother? Not yet. But I have brought your daughter a present. Does she like reading?"

"My Maria – of course. She has to. She has to become professore – like you. Next generation must do well, no? Maria! Where is that girl?"

Maria was finally located, dress stained, socks trailing down to her ankles, shoes scruffy – a plump girl with red cheeks and her mother's sunken eyes. She grabbed the package, tore off its wrapper, grimaced at the junior illustrated edition of "Pride and Prejudice" and ran off to her friends who had begun a round of "passing the cushion" on the front lawn. Beatrice saw the book get tossed onto a table amidst a pile of empty dishes and glasses.

Hercules blushed and shrugged. "Children!" He grinned sheepishly. "Miss Betty, you look very beautiful today."

Now it was her turn to blush. She had worn her hair scraped back in a pony tail and put on a white summer cotton dress and sandals. Casual but elegant was how she had wanted to be, to shed her stuffy university image. And Hercules appreciated it. She felt his eyes boring through her dress.

He also mercifully rescued her from embarrassment by waving his hand across the yard. "All my customers."

"And I thought you did all this handyman work only for me." She tried to be coy, but his tone was serious.

"You see, Miss Betty – my real family – my older brothers and sisters, they are all in-a Guelph. In the farm we bought-a when we come to this country. But after a while I get-a restless. I study everything – electrical, plumbing, carpentry. Then I come-a to Toronto because I wanted something different. So I start with this neighbourhood ah, doing small jobs. Now I have so much work and many loyal customers. They are like-a my family."

An old woman in black came out of the house. Beatrice wondered where she had been hiding – in the basement? Hercules immediately left the barbecue and walked over to help her down the steps to the yard. He pulled up a chair and sat her down, placing a glass and a plate of food on a table next to her. The old woman just stared and mumbled something to him.

When he returned to the barbecue, he apologized. "My mamma – she is deaf and going blind. She came this year from Italy. My brothers and sisters don't want her at the farm because she is too much trouble they say. So I look-a after her."

"And your wife doesn't mind?"

"Ah, my wife – Anna is from my mother's village. My mamma arranged the marriage and I brought-a Anna to Canada twelve years ago."

A carafe of wine came out from the house and the guests eagerly lapped it up. Another soon emerged. Beatrice was light-headed after her second glass and feeling bold. She sat next to the old woman, whose trembling hands had by now littered the ground around her with crumbs. Beatrice tried to make conversation in spite of the handicaps. All she received backs were grunts and burps as Hercules' mother digested her food.

Beatrice was about to excuse herself and leave, when the old woman croaked in a raspy voice, "His name – Luigi. Hercules, only for-a the business." Then she crooked a frail finger and Beatrice leaned over. The old woman whispered sharply in her ear. "Luigi – he is good boy. You be careful." A chill ran down Beatrice's back; she mumbled something and quickly made her getaway without looking back.

After a couple of forced conversations with the other guests, Beatrice got bored; the neighbours were obviously wary of her superior intellectual air and only replied when spoken to. She ambled over to Hercules once more. She realized that he had been glancing her way all the time she was mingling.

Hercules skewered a large long sausage sizzling on the grill and held it out to her. "Ah, Miss Betty – for you – the finest Italiana spicy sausage. Your plate, please."

That's when her boldness got the better of her. She looked into his eyes as she opened her mouth to take the sausage directly in, the plate dangling uselessly from her hand. The taste was sharp and the sensation fiery hot; she could not bite without burning herself. Instead she worked the sausage back and forth in her mouth, watching his intake of breath, the parting of his lips in a half smile, half grunt. It was an exhilarating and dangerous game and she could feel his excitement mounting in heart-pounding tempo with her own, as the sausage slid inside her mouth. She only stopped when she heard the scream. Beatrice broke away and spun around to see Anna, hand to her mouth, the food tray falling from her other hand and spilling its contents on the ground. Everyone was staring at Anna, but Anna was staring at *them*.

"Scusi," Hercules dropped the sausage as if it had burned him, and hurried over to his wife who had left everything as it was, turned on her heel and rushed indoors.

*   *   *

She stayed away from the Olivetti's and Hercules for a few months after that. She did not offer him any more work during that time either. And she kicked herself for behaving like a tramp.

Then Hercules' mother died and the neighbourhood filled with well-wishers coming and going to pay their respects. Beatrice thought it best to show up for the funeral at least. She was surprised to see Anna in an advanced stage of pregnancy, which accounted for something more than crying as the cause of her swollen face. For a moment the daughter-in-law looked like the chief mourner in the family. Hercules, though sombre and bowed, raised his eyes to Beatrice, the look of gratitude on his face evident.

"Grazie" he said.

"Putana!" Anna hissed from next to him. Hercules blushed and Beatrice felt her legs nearly give way. She staggered to the end of the line, ran into the washroom, and cried her eyes out. When she had recovered her composure, she left by the rear door, and rushed home.

She focused on her work and tried to put men out of her mind. Research held her attention and her interest, and they sent her away to Paris for six months on an exchange. The paper she delivered at the end of that period was very well received and she was invited to join an international group of scholars doing research into feminist movements in history. The French professors found her intellectually stimulating; some even wanted to go to bed with her and were blatant in their intentions. She found them objectionable and turned down all overt offers.

It was almost a year after the barbecue that she next met Hercules. Actually he came to her door.

He looked thinner with patches of grey at his temples. He had an apologetic look. "Miss Betty, sorry to disturb-a you," he started tentatively. She opened the door and a wave of emotion overcame her. She held herself from reaching out and embracing him. He shuffled and paid her compliments on how well she looked and how much he had missed working for her.

She decided to be business-like and hide behind the armour that had protected her so well in life and, in particular, during her recent sojourn in France.

"What can I do for you, Hercules? Is your family well?"

"They are-a well. My new little bambina, Sofia – she was born with the Down's syndrome."

"Oh dear, I am so sorry to hear that."

"It is okay. That is-a my cross, Miss Betty. I come to ask if you have any work for me. I am-a needing some extra money now – too many expenses. And with my bambina …"

"I understand. Well, the driveway needs repair. I was thinking of doing it next year. What do you think?"

His eyes lit up. "Oh, for sure you need to do it this year Miss Betty. I will work out a good-a price for you."

She felt relieved that she could help. The repair got underway that summer. She watched as Hercules and his assistant dug, cleaned, laid new rubble, stamped, spread the new coat of asphalt, sealed and transformed her driveway from a patchwork of cracks to a faultless blacktop that restored the rest of the property to its due elegance. Studying him at work, she realized how much she had missed him.

The evening the driveway was completed, when the assistant had left and Hercules was putting his tools away, she decided to get to the point. She was dressed in a pair of shorts and a bikini top, to make the best of the sweltering day.

She squatted on the front porch, feeling the humidity ooze out of her skin. The sun was setting and the street deserted. Hercules was lighting a cigarette, that far-away look on his face.

"Hercules, are you happy with your life?"

He raised an eyebrow. Then he smiled. "But of course, Miss Betty. Canada is a great country."

"Let me be more explicit – are you happy with your wife?"

He looked taken aback at her directness. He cleared his throat.

"My Anna, well she is a good wife. She take care-a the children, the house. She take-a care of my momma, God bless her soul. What can I be unhappy about?"

"You're too much in a mould, Hercules. People like you will never change from one generation to the next."

"But Miss Betty – what else can a man like-a me do? The mould, as-a you call it, it is also my… stability, no?"

"You fail to see what is around you." She felt her voice rising. "Have I never been any thing more to you than an employer?"

"But you are Professore. What can a man like me do but-a serve you?"

She rose from the steps, disgust in her face. "Go back to your life then. And send me the bill when you have finished the work. Good night."

She stalked into her bedroom. Suddenly everything was oppressive and she felt sweaty and dirty – a like a whore, a putana! She tore off her top and walked bare-chested into the washroom, only to come face to face with Hercules who had followed her indoors.

They froze in the passageway, he a helpless look on his face, she a look of annoyance that instantly turned to shock.

She clapped her hands to her breasts. "How dare you follow me?"

"No Miss Beatrice – this is not-a as you think. I come to say I am-a sorry." He averted his eyes with great effort.

She wanted to press those tantalizing breasts to his face, force his attentions on her, feel his warm big calloused hands moving all over her skin. Instead, she said, "Get out! Now!" She slammed the door to the washroom and broke into tears.

* * *

The next twenty years flew by. Nothing tugged her heart-strings as much as what had happened on that summer's day when the driveway was finished. If these intervening years should ever be subject to study, researchers would note two distinct phases: promiscuous and bored.

The first phase began when she succumbed to offers from male admirers at the university, hitherto kept at arms length. Married men, middle-aged and looking for a spark in their lives before they descended into decline. Men she could use, wield power over, and dispose of when the relationship became tedious. No one would talk, as discretion had to be maintained at all times. Her married lovers had more to lose than she.

The dean of the faculty was both the best and the worst conquest; in fact, he had to have her because lesser faculty had already had their turn. He was nearing retirement; he golfed, gardened, skied, sailed and rode his bicycle to work daily to prove his stamina. He was boring in bed, but she strung him along and boosted his ego. He arranged for conferences where they could go off together and jump into the sack between business sessions.

Then the dean had a fatal heart attack on one of those trips, while he was demonstrating how he could make love non-stop for three hours: an art he had apparently learned but never practiced with his wife who preferred quickies and sleep. At the 45-minute mark, in the middle of a spurt of renewed and accelerated thrusting, he clutched his heart and fell dead across her body.

The fallout was embarrassing; professional networks that had once boosted her ascendant career now did their best to drag her through the mud. She decided that early retirement from academia was in the cards. Thankfully, the likes of Hercules would never discover her secrets, for he could never enter these circles.

Leaving the university, and after a year of travel on a generous severance package, she joined the provincial government as a policy advisor and entered her boring phase. The policy papers she wrote were her best work, but they took several years to move through the echelons of power, often dying somewhere en-route. After a while she began taking lengthy tea and lunch breaks, read books at her desk, and yet people said she was doing a terrific job. She began writing a novel about an impossible romance between a handyman and an academic. She couldn't finish the manuscript; her ending kept changing.

She went off men again when she started forgetting their names. Her concentration at work started to go and she decided to get a medical check-up. The A word – albeit early symptoms - alarmed her. She retired again, to her home this time, finding solace in watching Hercules at work maintaining the house whenever he came over. She focused her efforts on playing the piano with increasingly arthritic hands and continued to write several possible new endings to her unfinished novel.

*　*　*

Hercules leaves his house at exactly 10 o'clock. He has risen early because he feels the day has lots of promise, despite the cold weather. He follows these routines now or else his day gets messed up.

In the hallway, he pauses to look at the family pictures: Maria, married now with three children; her husband beats her occasionally, especially when he is drunk, but for the most part they are a stable family, and Maria is the only one who visits regularly; Giovanna, single and in the convent, wanting to be a nun – he never understood that shy quiet girl; and poor Sofia dead at 15, so badly deformed, perhaps it was a good thing. He looks at the last picture he has of Anna. She packed on the weight before the cancer tore through her body two years ago – Anna, a loving mother, but a jealous wife with a fiery temper. *The good God gives and the good God takes.* His mamma had always told him not to expect everything in life; you kept alive by striving for a perfection that never comes.

He made that mistake of expectation with his mamma: brought her to Canada and realized her final dream of being re-united with the family. Wanting to make her life perfect at last. What did she do? She died!

Out of habit, he kisses the miraculous medal of the Virgin as he leaves the house. He has carried the medal around his neck since his childhood. He attributes to its supernatural powers the number of times he has been saved from accidents while at work, even the sparing of his life from the deadly stroke that felled him two years ago.

He pauses outside, a fit of indecision overtaking him, wondering whether he should take an alternative route; going past Miss Betty's house sends a chill down his spine. But it is the shortest route, and today, with ice on the sidewalks, he does not want to push his luck. He leans on his cane and pushes off, the right leg nearly useless. *It's a crazy day to go out.* But he gets crazy sitting indoors all day too.

He enjoys these outings, except for the cold – down to the bus stop at the bottom of the street and then to the social club where he and his retired buddies play rummy and poker for the small stakes their pensions can afford. It passes the time, and he has lots of it these days since he stopped working. Thank God he was sixty-six and could turn to government assistance when the stroke hit. Otherwise, he would have continued working. *What else can a man do when all his family has left him?*

As he nears Miss Betty's, he wonders whether he will see her in the window today and if she will wave at him. He looks forward to that wave – but only that. He doesn't know what got into her that last time after the funeral. Imagine, lying naked on his bed! When Maria dropped him home, there she was, Miss Betty, in his bed – the bed he had shared with Anna for thirty-five years – stark naked with a faraway look in her eyes.

Maria had screamed and said, "That crazy professor bitch!" and ran off to call the police. It had frightened him. He was under a lot of pressure that time, with Anna's passing, and then with Miss Betty. He got his stroke that same week.

Not that he didn't have his share of dalliances during his day. During his many house-calls. But they were all bored stay-at-home housewives, like Anna, and he understood how to seduce them. He had been discrete and kept those activities away from the neighbourhood, where chatty neighbours would have got word back to Anna. His lip curls at the memory; they had been good episodes; fed his ego and kept his libido in tune. But Miss

Betty was different; she was like the lady on the medal around his neck, to be worshipped from afar – distant, aloof – never to be conquered.

He nears Miss Betty's house. It looks run-down now – he hasn't been able to do any work on it since his stroke. This is the other reason he is reluctant to pass by; the beautiful nook he has renovated and maintained over the years for his unattainable Madonna, is falling apart. It saddens him.

There she is – in the window – looking at him. She raises her hand and waves and he pauses and waves back. She is still beautiful; as beautiful, as the day he first laid eyes on her struggling to unpack her books. But they are from two different worlds even though they live down the same street. And now she is going strange in her head and it is just the time when someone should help her, but here he is, stricken himself. Two souls destined never to be in the same orbit.

As he passes, a nagging thought that has been growing in intensity over the last few days, stops him. Why is he running away? He is widowed. She is single. They love each other, always have. What silly notion still keeps them apart? The old ones – class, education, Anna, religious values? But none of these matter any more. Class: she is retired, so is he; they are now of the same class – senior citizens. Education: that does not matter any more either, for half the time Miss Betty does not remember anything she has learned. Anna: she is dead. Religion: they are too old for adultery anymore, and no one said companionship is sinful. No, he has bound himself in a stupid notion. Stupid! Is it too late to turn back? He turns around, sucks in his breath, and walks back to her. *Go quickly idiot, before you change your mind again. You have wasted too much time already.* He quickens his pace, looking only at Miss

Betty framed in the bay window. His good leg slips on the ice, the bad one cannot compensate, and he starts to fall. Another silent voice admonishes him on his downward journey to the pavement - *Idiot, why did you not leave things alone – didn't your mamma teach you?*

*   *   *

She sees him come down the street and rises to take her place at the window and wave. This is the highlight of her day. He has lost his strength since the illness and relies heavily on his cane, his shoulders stooped, lips hanging from where the stroke deadened nerves. His decline, hers and that of her house, are interminably linked.

Her mind begins to wonder at that point and she knows this is the dangerous part. So far the memories have come easily, but when the "muddles" happen, she does not know where she is or what she is doing. She sits down, takes the papers she has just signed and forces herself to focus on the print – meaningless commitments to live in a nursing home for the rest of her days. But that does not help and she slips away.

She is back at that time when she knew that she had to have Hercules before it was too late for both of them. His wife had just died, and who better to replace Anna than herself? She left the house in her muddled state and headed over to the Olivettis that day. That's all she remembers. They later told her awful things in the hospital; that she had been naked on his bed; that Hercules had covered her with a blanket while Maria called 911.

111

The muddle starts to clear and she sees Hercules has walked to the end of the street. And he is turning now. She holds her breath. He is coming to her. After all these years he is coming to her! But then he starts to fall. He is falling on the slippery sidewalk. Even before his head makes contact with the concrete, she is jumping out of her chair and running for the door.

*   *   *

The wind whips her, and she nearly stumbles, boots untied, a winter coat unbuttoned and hastily thrown over her housecoat. She makes it down to the sidewalk by sheer will. The street is deserted at this time of the late morning – school kids and office workers long gone and ensconced in their cozy workplaces.

Hercules is lying on the sidewalk, a trail of blood trickling from a gash on his head.

"Oh, my darling!" There is no point in holding back any more. She cradles him to her breast and puts her lips to his temples; a weak pulse still beats.

A car brakes nearby and the driver sticks his head out of the window. "Need some help?"

She is too engrossed in trying to revive Hercules and does not answer. The man gets out of his car and sizes up the situation quickly. "Madam – this looks pretty serious. We'd better call an ambulance." He digs inside his pocket and fishes out a cell phone.

"No!" Beatrice manages finally. "We have to get him inside the house first."

"But he needs medical help."

"Please… please help me get him inside. He will die in this cold."

The man hesitantly puts the cell phone back in his pocket and grabs Hercules under the arms. They manage to half carry, half drag Hercules between them into the house.

"This way. To the bedroom." Beatrice, still in her boots and coat, leads the way.

The man lays Hercules down on her bed with a grunt. "Now we have to call an ambulance." He gets out his cell phone once more and dials 911.

Beatrice removes Hercules' shoes and pulls a blanket over him.

"What address do I give?" the man interrupts.

She cannot remember now. "I… I don't know."

The man looks at her quizzically; sees the stress on her face, the anguish when she looks down at Hercules. "Don't worry ma'am. You tend to your husband. I'll get the number from outside." He leaves by the side door.

They are alone together, at last. She is curiously excited – like the last time, when she was in a bedroom alone with him. But that had been another room. She starts to get muddled again. She is back in that room: the gaudy red and yellow curtains; the bright orange bedspread – Hercules and Anna's bed. Something had driven her there. The urge to consummate a desire that had dogged her most of her adult life; a desire that could not be fulfilled by the men with whom she'd had casual sex. Even though she had imagined Hercules in all those encounters, it was never quite right. She had those trysts precisely because she could not have him. And there she was in Hercules's room waiting for him just as soon as he came home from Anna's funeral – to comfort and solace him. He had held her that time, not with desire, but with gallantry – trying to protect her from herself. He had placed a blanket over her nakedness, rejecting her body that she had finally offered to him.

Her muddle starts to clear and she can make out her own bed, handed down from parents to an only spoilt child, and this time it is she who has placed a blanket over him. The blood from his head has spread on to her embroidered pillow. *This time he will not reject me.*

"You are mine now, Hercules," she says, holding him in her arms. "Finally, after all these years, I get to have you."

He is trying to say something. She thinks he is shaking his head, forming the word "No" even at this last pass.

"No? Why no, my love?" She is hurt and holds him tighter. He struggles but is weak and she can sense the life force leaving him.

Finally, he shudders and gives in, allowing her to wrap him inside her clothing, her warm, shrivelled breast against his cheek. A smile plays upon his cold lips, "Ah Cara Mia – if you will-a have me… then …"

As the sound of a wailing ambulance enters her consciousness, she forces herself to give him what life she has, holding on to a thread of hope that she be joined with him, either in this life, or the next.

8

The Virtual Guy

It was on the day of the snowstorm about a year ago that I received the first message. My secretary, who is a New Age convert, would have called it synchronicity – one of those buzzwords aging yuppies are embracing wholesale these days. The business-class ticket had qualified me for a breather in the frequent-flyer lounge at La Guardia, while waiting for my flight back to Toronto. After a week of gruelling meetings, I was heading back to an empty apartment and some peace and quiet. Things were not going to be the same on the work front come next year, so moments of stillness were little gems in these times.

He was in his late thirties, had short, spiked hair and wore thick lenses. A nervous twitch jumped out of him periodically as he focused maniacally on his laptop in the adjacent pod of lounge chairs. Red lights beamed from the wireless modem as he punched the laptop's keys. His concentration was distracting, so I tried ignoring him and looked outside at the tarmac. Snow was beginning to fall, and the skies looked pregnant with a heavy load of the white stuff. Already "cancelled" notices were up for some of the shorter-haul flights.

"They'll shut down the airport soon," he said suddenly looking up. Before I could reply, he thrust the laptop at me. "See – I'm dialled into the satellite pictures. She's moving very fast – the storm. Should be hitting us in about half hour."

Just then the announcement for "all flight cancellations until further notice," went out on the PA system.

Another hassle to deal with. All the mounting troubles in my life came flooding in. A recent divorce with property matters to settle, a daughter demanding money and attention, a son constantly spinning get-rich schemes, a changing workplace, and now a shutting-everything-down storm.

Cell phones snapped open all over the lounge. I did not carry one of those gadgets, but wished I had one now. I slid the payphone over, swiped my credit card and called my secretary in Toronto. Let someone else deal with this. Her voicemail announced that due to the bad weather, the office had closed early. Suddenly I realized how helpless I was. I went over to the reception and asked the airline attendant if she could re-book my flight.

"There's none leaving tonight, sir,"

"But I have no hotel reservations!"

"I'll see what I can do, sir."

After fifteen minutes, she gave up. "Everything's fully booked, sir."

I returned to my bags and plunked down in the armchair. People were putting their cell phones away and leaving the lounge – maybe they had found alternative arrangements. I needed a drink. I went over to the bar, but it was shutting down too, "due to the inclement weather." I managed to salvage the last beer.

The guy with the spiked hair was powering down his laptop.

"I guess we're stuck here, eh?" I said.

"I've managed to get a hotel room."

"You did? How?"

"Booked it online. It's not much, but it will do – it's on the other side of town."

"Good luck getting there in this weather."

"I booked a rental car too. And if we hurry, we can get it before they give it out to another deserving soul. Come on. I'll give you a ride."

Gratefully, I followed him out.

*　*　*

"Take the next turn on your right." My companion had asked me to drive while he used a satellite map system on his laptop to guide us to our destination. All I could see were white streets, and cars looming out of nowhere. The yellow cabs, synonymous with this city, had all but disappeared. Only crazy people like us were on the road tonight.

"Is it White Horse Street or White Horn?"

"White Horse. And its 1.7 miles down this road to a left at Charles Avenue and we're home at the first set of lights."

It was a sleazy looking no-name brand motor hotel. I had no idea how he had found it on the Internet, but I wasn't complaining.

"It was the last available room – but I'm okay to share."

"Listen, I don't even know your name – I'm Don." I said as we swung into the motel parking lot.

"George."

The night clerk wanted an extra ten bucks for the second guest in the room. The reception area was smoky and filled with people sitting around with bags – stuck like us. "You can get dinner until 8:00 p.m. in the restaurant," the clerk said.

"Sounds like a plan," George said. Neither of us was in the mood for any more driving that night.

After dumping our bags in a room that smelled of old smoke and cover-up air freshener – thankfully it had two double beds – we went down to the restaurant. For such an out-of-the-way place, it was full. We managed to get a table after half an hour, a couple of bottles of beer and the special of the day – New York sandwiches – everything else had been gobbled up by the sudden rush of patrons.

"I don't drink alcohol – you can have my beer. Figured you'd need another, and I don't think there'll be any left by the time we get to a second round," George said.

He settled for water and I was grateful for the insurance of another beer – a good companion on a night like this.

By the time the second beer hit the spot, my third, if you count the one at the airport, I was beginning to feel less uptight.

"Where's home?" I asked.

"Oh, most places, these days – hotels. I do get back to Chicago, which is my base, once in awhile. Where are you from?"

"Toronto. What's your line of work?"

"Consulting. Software services. How about you?"

"Manufacturing. Family?"

"No. Well, sort of. I'm divorced," he said.

"So am I. Awful isn't it?"

"It was the best thing for me and my family. My work takes me away too much."

"Was the worst thing for me. Financially draining. Kids are emotionally fucked up now."

"Do you travel often?" he asked after a long pause.

"Not much. We opened a plant in New York recently – trying to capture the US market. The Canadian business isn't so hot anymore. I'm heading up the project. I might be traveling more until we're fully operational."

"I spend about one hundred and twenty nights out of the year in hotel rooms. Time zones are the hardest to work around. I get indigestion every time I'm in New Delhi because I eat dinner when I should be having breakfast."

"I can see why you prefer to be single."

"It wasn't my choice – it was karma. Consulting was the logical path after my MBA."

When we got back to the room he pulled out his laptop again.

"I guess you'll be busy for the rest of the evening, eh?" I said, relieved in a way that I did not have to keep him company. All that beer had made me drowsy.

"I hope you don't mind. I'll try not to be too noisy – but it's going to be opening time in India right now and I have a project there that's at a dicey stage – I need to spend a couple of hours online trying to sort things out."

"Go ahead. I'll watch a bit of TV and get some shut eye, I guess."

Except for news of the storm blacking out most airports on the east coast being the big story, the TV was uninteresting – a few murders and some corporate scandals. Same-old, same-old.

My mind drifted to the remnants of my family and the recent call I had received from Trish, twenty one, in her final year at university, wanting a car for her birthday. A car, when I was in debt to my eyeballs, thanks to her older brother Brad, the hot-shot investment broker and his fiasco of a get-rich quick scheme. "Let's go dot.com Dad, you can't go wrong." We even took a second mortgage on the house to fuel some of those new enterprises that were increasing in wealth by the day. Brad was already a millionaire – on paper – and I was trying to catch up and justify my thirty years of plodding in the stodgy manufacturing sector. I knew nothing about the dot.com industry; heck I couldn't even handle e-mail, but the growth opportunities had been tempting. When it all burst, my wife, Jane decided to leave me because I was a failure. Brad disappeared, nursing his wounds somewhere in Alberta, and the house was repossessed. And now Trish, asking for a car – I guess money drove my family. Money equalled success and love.

I must have dozed off when I heard giggling. Opening an eye I looked across at George. He was animated over what looked like a computer game on his machine. He had connected a joystick to the laptop and was wearing a headset that was plugged into the telephone.

"Great Joey – you got me that time didn't you?"

I got up and studied my roommate. His screen was partitioned into four quadrants – the game had now been placed into one, there was an online dialogue playing in another. What looked like an e-mail was in the third, and a spreadsheet filled the last screen. And George was popping in and out of each of them as he spoke on the phone.

"Its bed time now Joey – we'll play again tomorrow, okay? Love you lots! Goodnight!"

The game screen went blank, filled immediately by another.

I saw his face in the glimmer of the laptop. When he flipped to the dialogue screen he was all warmth and tenderness. Every time he hit enter and popped over to the e-mail or spreadsheet he was a study of focus and concentration with the nervous twitch returning.

I looked at my watch; it was just after 11:00 p.m. I wondered how long this would be going on. Just then, he looked away from the screen and rubbed his eyes. I tried to keep my eyes shut but I guess he saw me move.

"I won't be much longer now, Don. Just waiting on an urgent e-mail from India to come through."

"That's a lot of transactions you're processing. Sorry, I did not mean to pry."

"Oh, no problem. I was playing a video game online with my son. It's our daily ritual of keeping in touch wherever in the world I am. And I was on a chat line with my fiancée as well. It helps with the work/life balance thing."

"I thought you said you chose to remain single?" I guess I was feeling envious. After Jane left it had been singles clubs for me and the occasional triple X video when I was too tired to be looking my smartest just to get the ashes hauled.

"This time around I specified my partner's requirements – I needed someone who could accommodate my schedule. My fiancée is also a consultant – we spend most of our time online – in fact that's how we met. Our only shared base is Chicago, where we both live."

"And that's where you two spend the other of the 245 days in the year when you are not traveling?"

"Make that about 100 days – my fiancée also travels, even

more than I do, and our schedules don't always coincide. But she understands my life. We are constantly in contact. I call her my guardian angel."

The screens started to close on his laptop.

"You're pretty good with that machine," I said.

He scratched his head and smiled. The nervous tick was gone. "Well, I had to train myself. When this becomes your only lifeline with the rest of the world, you learn it pretty fast. And you respect it too. Sorry, that I've hogged the phone line – these hotels don't have dual lines. Do you want to call your family, perhaps?"

"My family doesn't know where the heck I am right now, and frankly I don't know if they really care. Except perhaps for Trish, my daughter."

"I'm sorry to hear that. At least your daughter cares."

"She needs a car for her birthday – that's why she cares."

As he was silently stowing his laptop, I felt like talking, even if he was not listening. "I guess when you build a family with money as the overriding metric of success, you get my kind of problems."

"You know, I can't focus on money – it's so illusory. One day I've got plenty in my forecast, then the jobs dry up and I've got lean periods. So I try not to think about it."

"I drilled it into my kids. Tried to instil the same discipline I was raised with. Had to put myself through college – student loans and all that. I struggled all the way from engineer to office manager, then regional manager, and they recently made me a director in the company."

"At the same firm?"

"We don't hop around too much in my line of business."

"At least you've had employment security."

"But I never could make the big time and establish my own company. Salaried employees, you know. Then I had a chance a couple of years ago, but it didn't pan out. Lost all I had."

"That's what I felt when I had to give up my family."

"Sent my kids to private schools – paid a lot of money for it. I wanted to give them the leg-up I never had. But they haven't done much with it. Now all they want is more."

"Maybe what they *need* is 'less'. Joey really looks forward to his 'daily hour' with me online."

I pondered his words for awhile as images of "Who Wants to be a Millionaire," flashed by. I switched off the TV.

"Well, best get some shut eye," I said. "I guess we can't solve all the world's problems tonight."

"We sure can't," he said taking out his toiletries and heading for the bathroom. "But we sure can choose our response to them, huh?"

I had a fitful sleep that night, while George was snoring minutes after he hit the pillow. I dreamt of Trish crying in the park as someone had taken her toy away from her, and of Jane pointing accusatory fingers at me and saying it was my fault. The usual dreams, embellished with new ones of airplanes crashing in the snowstorm; of computer nerds who did not have the right stuff to run their dot.coms, now becoming my best friends.

When I woke it was still dark. The clock read 5:30 a.m. George was already hunched over his laptop. I put on the coffee machine.

"Coffee?"

He was absorbed by whatever was coming from that screen, and probably did not hear me. I repeated my request, louder and he looked up, looking a bit crestfallen.

"Oh, yes, please."

I switched on the TV. The storm had blown over and the airport would be operating again.

"Good news. We can get out today," I announced.

"Yes. Unfortunately my news is not that good. I got that e-mail finally. The contract in India has fallen through. I guess I am into another lean period now."

I handed him the streaming mug. "Sorry to hear that. How much was that deal worth?"

"Oh, a couple of hundred grand over the next nine months."

"That's a big one." That was about what I lost when I split the dwindled family fortune with Jane.

"There'll be others." Then he smiled. "You know, the good news is that I don't have to go to India next week, and Jennifer, my fiancée is back in Chicago. So it's a great outcome after all."

"Well, we'd best be off to the airport – the place will be like a zoo. Getting a seat back will be a challenge."

Then I saw his twinkling smile. "Unless… unless that is …"

"You bet. I booked you on Air Canada at 10:00 a.m. and mine's at 9:45. Booked it while you were asleep. We'd better get a move on!"

*   *   *

We got separated just after the security check. He was ahead of me while the woman in uniform suddenly took an interest in my heavy Canadian winter shoes. I saw George waving, saying his flight to Chicago was boarding; and then he was gone in a flurry of bags, guards and passengers, while the security woman ran my shoes through the X-ray machine a second time. When I got to my gate, I phoned Trish from a payphone nearby.

"Oh, Dad – we were wondering about you in the storm and all." She sounded guilty.

"That's funny. There were no messages from you in my voice-mail box," I said dryly. "But listen, kiddo, I've been thinking – about the car."

"Yes?" Anticipation crackled though the line.

I let the silence hang for awhile. I looked over at the Air Canada flight that had commenced boarding, dishevelled people jostling each other to get through the gate. Didn't they know that from this point on they would be matched to a seat on board?

"Daddy, I'm waiting …" Trish's voice had taken on a familiar coyness.

"Oh, yes. I've decided *not* to buy you the car. You've got to make it on your own, honey. And you don't need a car to do it. You'll make it only if you want to."

I put down the phone just as she was going into her usual tirade of nobody in this world loving her, and headed for my flight.

*   *   *

As I mentioned, that all happened a year ago. I did not see George again after that. He had given me his business card, but like many of those pieces of paper we exchange in life, I misplaced it somewhere between LaGuardia and Toronto. Trish graduated after all. She got a job as a marketing assistant in a financial services company downtown and doesn't talk to me anymore. I hope she'll come around in time. Brad finally got in touch; knowing my aversion to e-mail, he sent me a fax saying he was sorry for what had happened with the dot.coms but there was this new energy venture in northern Alberta and would I be interested? I wished him luck and said that if he made any money on it, could he send me some?

My project actually took off. I wasn't such a loser after all, Jane dear. In fact, it was so successful that within the year the company decided to move its operations to the United States. I got a memo last Monday saying that I could either re-locate or, given my long tenure and experience, work virtual from Canada as a consultant to the company. I'd succeeded in putting myself out of a job. New York was not a place I particularly wanted to live in at this stage of my life, and I was probably going to be useless working virtual. I was not very computer savvy; my secretary organized everything for me, including printing important e-mail so I could handwrite short replies on them; and I liked ordering people around. How the heck could I do that at the end of a telephone or computer terminal? After thirty years with the same company, this looked like the end of the road for me.

That's when I began to think about George and that night we spent in New York together. Now there was a guy who knew how to make this virtual thing work to his advantage. I thought about him a lot this past week. I wished I had kept his business card.

My secretary stuck her head in. "There's a man on the line from Turkey — someone named Angelis. He says he's been trying to e-mail you for the last several days, but you have not responded. Come to think of it, I've seen a couple of his come through."

I couldn't remember when I had last logged into my computer this week. I'd gotten pretty lazy, especially since the re-location notice had come out.

"If he's trying to sell us something, tell him I'm not interested."

"He thinks you're in some kind of trouble and wants to help. Are you?"

"Tell him to go mind his own troubles."

Then I sat up bolt upright. I had forgotten his last name. "No, don't hang up …" I was running out of the office, but she was already replacing the receiver.

"Was his first name, George?"

She looked perplexed, then beamed. "You must be getting synchronistic – how did you know?"

"Did he leave a phone number?"

"He was on a cell phone just boarding a transatlantic flight. He said he would be out of contact for about ten hours."

I ran back into my office to log onto the desktop. I had to shout back to her for the password, as I had changed it recently and already forgotten. "It's 'George'," she cooed back, "Remember? My, you really must have this George fellow on your mind!" I wish my secretary wasn't a happily married grandmother, because I could have run away with her right then and there – the woman took such good care of me in the office. And now, with the relocation, I was going to lose her too. Oh yes, the password – George - I'd changed it only last week but hadn't used the computer since. Last month it had been 'Trish.' Why did I have to change these bloody access codes every thirty days, anyway?

Sure enough, there were two e-mails sitting there from

George. My secretary had filed both in the "Miscellaneous Reading" folder, bless her heart!

The first, received five days ago, said that he was now on a project in Istanbul which was very exciting, and he got to travel home twice a month. He and Jennifer were planning to tie the knot in the spring. He had seen our company's relocation notice on an Internet news bulletin, etc, etc. Why this sudden communiqué, after almost a year? The second e-mail, sent only yesterday, was more ominous.

"Why are you silent? I *feel* you're in some dilemma, Don. Do write. It helps. – George"

Then it clicked. Things happen for a reason – like my secretary would preach to me every morning after her weekly new-age group meeting. Some, we mortals cannot fathom, but need to abide by. If she was right, change was in the air, and I hadn't been getting it. It had been coming since that stormy night in La Guardia. "It's that synchronicity thing, or whatever, Barb," I said out aloud to her.

I started writing. My typing was a halting two-finger symphony – but it would have to get faster in the days ahead.

I wrote only a short response, but that was enough.

"George – you just solved my dilemma. I'm going virtual! At least, I'm going to try. Thanks for being my guardian angel! – Don

P.S – What was that web site you met Jennifer at?"

9

New Homes, Old Loves

Arnold Bradley squinted and wobbled in the sunlight as he left his bungalow for the last time. He never looked back when he left a home, preferring to leave the ghosts, the experiences and the years behind, looking forward to new beginnings at the next destination. But today was different.

The openness of the outdoors gave him a temporary sense of insecurity. Despite the movers having taken most of his things away, the house was small enough to always have at least a wall within holding distance. He pressed down on the walking stick, which helped nowadays, for his step had slowed considerably, the right leg developing a random, involuntary jerk that threatened to topple his two-hundred-and-fifty pound body.

The limo was in the driveway and his regular driver, Pervez, wearing a navy blue sweater, held the door open and bowed. The air had turned nippy and the leaves a shade of rusted orange.

"Morning Pervez," Arnold's tone was bright, despite his doubts. The pills would hold him until about 3:00 p.m., when he'd need to take his nap, and then some more pills before dinner.

"Good morning, sir." There was a tone of regret in Pervez's voice. Perhaps he thought there would be no more hires for him, at least, not as regularly anymore. "Do you want to go directly sir?"

"No. I think I would like you to drive me around a bit. There are a few places I want to visit first."

"Very well, sir." Pervez's accent made it sound like, "Vary vall, sar."

When he was safely installed in the back seat, Arnold gave the driver the first address. Pervez raised his eyebrows, then nodded. It did not pay to question this eccentric old man who had money to spare for limo rides.

The Lincoln Town Car swept by a few side streets, took an arterial road for about fifteen minutes, then entered a newer subdivision and parked on the sidewalk next to a sprawling two-story house protected by an ornate fence and wrought iron gate.

Pervez clicked on his walkie-talkie to hand in his co-ordinates to Dispatch. "Sir, what destination shall I give them for this detour?"

"No need to be discreet, Pervez. Tell 'em it's my old home – one of them."

Arnold eased his bulk out of the back seat and leaned heavily on his cane. He shuffled over to the gate and tenderly ran his pudgy hands over it. He had installed this fence himself, twenty-five years ago, when his limbs had been wiry and flexible, after he moved into the big house behind the gate with Marguerite.

Yes, Marguerite – how would he remember her? In her forties – the best years – and the best of the women he married. Educated, elegant, she set him off during the banner years of his life, when the factory had moved into high gear with acquisitions and expansions pouring in; when he had stepped aside and let professional managers run things; when all he did was wine, dine, play golf, vacation and hobnob with the best of society, resulting only in more business coming his way. That was also when the weight began to pile on his softening body, for he'd been happy and felt invincible. Marguerite threw exquisite parties, superbly catered, the wines well chosen, always the best champagne and hors d'oeuvres; she magically picked perfect days for the outdoor functions. There never was a rained-out event.

He hobbled, sniffing like a dog looking for a break in the fence, and stared through a chink at the house. The new owners had filled in the pool and converted it into a tennis court. He had left a big mark in this house. He remembered every room; they had made love in each one. On the Persian rug in the living room, on the kitchen counter, on his work desk, in the library, in the music room on her piano, in the bedroom of course, and even on the pool deck – just for the hell of it. The sheer feeling of being in control of life had been exhilarating.

Standing here and remembering brought a surge of that exhilaration back. He realized that despite all the fun and frolic, he had been a success in business too, and Marguerite was the one he associated with that success.

"Let's go," he instructed Pervez, who was starting to doze.

"Ah, okay sir." Pervez scratched his head at the next address Arnold handed him. "Sir, this is about 100 kilometres away. You will be late for your appointment."

"I told them I'd be late. I've got the money, and you have the car. Drive."

Arguing was useless. Pervez nodded and put the car in gear. They headed out of the city, through the suburbs, out into the eastern townships along the lake. Then they headed north along a country road for about twenty-five kilometres.

"Go slow here," Arnold said. "I hardly recognize this area anymore. There were only farms once; now it's all residential."

"You used to live here too, sir?"

"Yes, a long time ago. This is where my first wife and I came after we got married – me to experiment, and she to run the bed and breakfast so we could put bread on the table."

The farm was now a subdivision of box-like bungalows, newly built, the lawns not even sodded yet. A sign said that a school would be opening here shortly. Arnold laughed silently. When he and Josie had come here, the closest school was a half-hour bus ride away. That's why Joey did not come home from school that day. *Bloody drunk driver on a country road!*

Josie, the only woman who had given him a child. Thin, hardworking, religious, with failing health, even though she got up daily to cater to farm-tour visitors who stopped in at the B&B. Joey, spirited, prankster, even when he was little – always running off and hiding in the woods until Arnold had to come and seek him out. Too young to be robbed of life at only eight years of age. Shoving aside the paramedics, Arnold had lifted the boy's battered body from the ditch he had been hurled into, and carried him to the ambulance. That had been the longest walk of his life. He'd shut children out of his life ever since.

"There used to be a farm house here," Arnold said to Pervez. "I was an agricultural scientist. We also planted corn and vegetables. But you don't make money with that stuff. Even then I saw farmers going the way of the dodo."

"Dodo, sir?" Pervez asked looking extremely puzzled. "Is that something you planted also?"

"No – it's an extinct bird – a figure of speech."

"Ah." But Pervez was still frowning. Arnold ignored him. He liked Pervez – a good sounding board.

"I found a technique for growing larger vegetables. Cross pollination and stuff. They call it genetic engineering these days."

"Ah, yes. If we could get genetic engineering in Pakistan, I wouldn't have come here, sir. Most of our food is imported and is very expensive. Couldn't feed my family. I even had a good government job – civil service."

"Yes, I know the drill. I hired a lot of scientists from the third world in my factory when I got into genetics full time. Didn't have a clue about where I was going, but I believed in its potential."

"You must have made a lot of money, sir."

"Yes, I did. But I lost the only things I loved. I got greedy, you see."

"A lot of greedy people in my country, also sir. Politicians are the worst."

"It's a human trait, Pervez, no matter where you live. Stay here, I am going to take a walk down that path."

But it was hard going. Just as he was out of sight of the driver, Arnold's leg jerked involuntarily on the downward slope of the path, sending him sprawling on the ground, smearing his khaki pants with soft green sludge from the wet grass.

He decided to sit there, until his legs regained their strength and the twitching stopped. *Got to increase the dosage.* He had walked down this path many times, with Josie in the early days of their marriage, building dreams of how the factory would be built immediately following his first research breakthrough. In later years, he had also stolen along this path at night to the white house on the hill by the boundary of his property – the Saunders' country residence, where Marguerite practiced her bohemian lifestyle, under the shelter of her parents' wealth and position in the county. There were always parties and people on the lawns of that sprawling mansion. Arnold used his field glasses to track her movements: flirting with male companions, married or single; supervising the waiters; moving fluidly from one group to the other, weaving swathes around their conversations and leaving them smiling and shaking their heads as she flitted on to the next group. He had decided then that she would be the ideal life-mate for him, once his inventions made money. Josie was not going to get him there; and after Joey had died, their love for each other became unsustainable.

He remembered the first time they were invited to the Saunders' residence for a cocktail party. Arnold had been in his element, aided by a couple of Scotches, postulating on how to increase yields per acre four-fold with the new grain formula he had patented. Marguerite looked at him with wide eyes; for once she hadn't been in control. Josie sat lost on the far side of the garden, her black dress pulled around her, sad eyes begging her husband to call it a night.

Arnold rolled onto his knees, garnering more patches on his pants, and hoisted himself up, praying his leg would not give way again. He leaned heavily on the walking stick until his head stabilized. *Need to check that blood pressure soon.* Once, they had rolled on this same grass, Marguerite and him, the night she had given up resisting involvement with a married man, and they had made love for the first time, under the stars, plunging him into the next phase of his life.

He made his way back slowly to the car. Pervez looked alarmed when he saw his passenger emerge over the hill.

"Sir, did you fall – have an accident?"

"Ah, it's nothing. Just a slip on the hill down there." But his entire leg was in pain.

"We should go, sir – no more detours."

"One more stop, Pervez. Remember I am paying the bill. Here, this is where I want you to take me now." Arnold was glad he had written these slips before setting out from the house.

Pervez frowned when he read the address. "This is back in the city – other side."

"Yes and you get to make a lot of money today. Drive on."

When they were midway to their destination and Arnold had managed to massage his leg as best as he could, he interrupted Pervez, who was heavily engaged in the Urdu news channel.

"Do you have a family, Pervez?"

"Uh? Oh, family?" Pervez was pulling himself away from the radio and appeared disconnected. Arnold repeated the question.

"Of course – sir – I will always have a family. My three daughters are all married. One married a doctor and has two children, the other an engineer and has one child, and the third just got married to an accountant."

"And your wife?"

"She is very well, sir. Eagerly awaiting more grandchildren."

"Did you ever cheat on your wife, Pervez?"

Pervez looked back slyly at Arnold, then quickly shifted and kept his eyes on the road ahead. "No, sir."

"You are sure?"

Pervez clenched and unclenched the wheel several times. "Well sir – maybe once in a while when Begum was in Pakistan visiting the relatives – you know she would go away sometimes for six months. Sometimes only, sir."

"You fucked around on your wife, eh?"

"Acha, sir – don't say it like that. We men also have urges, no? Must not keep everything inside. There is a widow in our community – she is very discreet. But nobody knows, sir. And if nobody knows, nobody will get hurt that way."

"They usually find out, Pervez. And, they get hurt."

Like he did when he couldn't get it up anymore for Olga. Olga – his Russian blonde, who was going to keep him forever young, but instead made him feel old; Olga, who insisted that he provide her "relief" with whomever, when he had lost his performance edge.

Many times he would walk into her room while she cavorted with a younger man, usually screened and found through the Internet, the same way Arnold had first found her.

He remembered how he had sweated, posting his profile on the Net. But it was the dawn of the new millennium – no one had time to hang around in bars to pick up chicks anymore. The good chicks no longer hung around the bars; they had all retreated to computer screens in the comfort of their homes where they could flirt with hungry, lonely men who pretended they were something they weren't.

Finally the pain and humiliation had been too much. Why was he – Arnold Bradley, scientist turned super industrialist, man of wealth, cuckolded by a woman nearly half his age? He threw her out.

But "the pogrom," as she called it, followed – the hounding by lawyers for alimony, share of assets, and on it went. A man cannot fight a battle on two fronts. When the Americans came calling to buy his firm, he resisted; when Olga sent in her lawyers for the separation agreement, he resisted. Then the Americans started luring away his scientists, and he couldn't produce variants to his mutant seeds to combat new soil pests that were emerging daily and eating commercial crops. Customers left in droves; the Americans laughed and withdrew their offer to buy for a while. "Sink, you asshole" was written subliminally in the last communiqué he received from them. Olga's lawyers persisted. That's when the night sweats started, and the involuntary jerks intensified, culminating in the massive heart attack.

"Yes, they do get hurt. Both sides." Arnold said, almost to himself.

They were back in the city, heading up Highway 427 on the west end. Before long they reached northern Mississauga, driving down streets of tall elms and willows.

"Here's the house. Stop on the other side."

"Sir – you used to live here, no? Only a few years ago. I remember the first time I came to pick you up was from here."

"Yes," Arnold nodded. That's when he had to give up driving. His leg had begun to twitch at embarrassing moments – like when he pushed down on the brake.

Pervez edged between two other cars alongside the curb. Arnold decided to stay put. Olga could be watching, if she wasn't getting laid somewhere else in the house.

"Not getting out, sir?"

"No – let's say, the environment is not conducive to it."

Marguerite had died suddenly – six months and she was gone with a brain tumour. Cancer is no respecter of people's ambitions or personal timetables. He was left a lonely old man of sixty-five, still physically fit, comfortably off with two factories exporting genetic secrets all over the world. Enter Olga, thirty-five, fresh from Russia, determined to make her mark and "out to please her man, in any which way she could", as her Internet profile said. And she did – the sex was incredible – Arnold felt like a twenty-five year-old. Not since Josie (until Joey was born), or Marguerite in their twenty years of marriage (until her sudden rapid decline) had he had such good sex. On scale, Olga topped the other two. And Arnold felt he was owed, having lost two wives already.

But then he hadn't counted on his own aging. At first there were the little blue pills to help him, but when his blood pressure got in the way, he could no longer take them. His normally nubile phallus rolled over and went dead in no time, but Olga was as hungry as ever.

"The rise and fall of man," Arnold said aloud.

"What's that sir?"

"This house reminds me of my decline."

"But it's a very nice big house. The best we have seen today."

Pervez was right. This house had cost about three-quarter million and was probably now worth double that, even if it was in the burbs. Swimming pool, twice the size of the one in the house he'd shared with Marguerite, four-car garage – two spots to accommodate the boat they rarely took out because Olga suffered from motion sickness (funny, she never got sick being rocked in bed), even a stable for the horse he had bought her. What an extravagance!

It was also the house in which he had left the smallest footprint, retreating finally to a room on the east end when Olga and her male guests became too boisterous and intrusive.

When he left her the house, he was literally bankrupt. The

company had imploded. He caved in to the Americans: sold them all his patents at fire sale prices and shut down the factory. He went to live in the little rental bungalow in the east end of the city; four more years of living in solitude, writing his memoirs and putting his residual finances in order. There was just enough money to make one final bequest. He laughed when he remembered where his name had appeared as a donor in the old days – practically in every major charity in the city. Now there was only enough to take care of himself modestly, taking it easy for the sake of his heart and feeling the stiffness creep over his body, and the loss of control of his muscles that resulted in him jerking around at the whims and fancies of some unknown ghost he must have displeased over the course of his life. He wondered if that ghost was Josie. She certainly had cause for grievance – he had dumped her for Marguerite and had not given her anything in the way of spousal support because he had been heavily mortgaged in starting up his company. But Josie was dead now, ostensibly of a heart attack at the age of sixty, but old friends told him she had died of a broken heart, and he did not probe further – just buried himself in Marguerite.

Ironically, Marguerite went soon after that too. Would Marguerite have been angry? No, she was his one true love, snatched from him like a piece of candy waved in front of a kid's nose and taken away. Was Olga angry? No, she was laughing out the other end of her face at this old dodderer who had married her to regain his youth – limp dick that he was!

A man appeared in the window of the house. A curtain flapped and went down. Then a woman's silhouette embraced the man, pulling him away from the window.

Arnold sighed. "Let's go. I am ready for my appointment now." He was glad to have faced his ghosts today. A few more rides like this, and he should be rid of them; if he could bring himself to take more rides.

They were both quiet as the limo plodded through downtown traffic. The towers had changed the landscape from when he was young. But was he afraid of change – of the changes coming his way at the end of this journey? He wondered. No, he was more frightened of falling downstairs in his little east-end bungalow because he couldn't trust his heart or limbs anymore.

"What will you do when you retire, Pervez?"

"Oh, I can't wait for the day, sir. My wife and I are going back to Pakistan. We have bought a house there."

"And you'd leave your children behind in Canada?"

"This country is for them, sir. I came here too late. My home is in Pakistan. My children will visit."

"And your wife – will she be happy going back?"

"She will be happy where I am, sir. Her place is with me. Without a husband, a woman is nothing, sir, in my world."

Arnold looked out the window again. What different worlds they inhabited. Would it all have been different if he had stayed married to Josie, cheating a bit on the side now and then like Pervez? At least, they would have grown old together. Instead, he had outgrown his wives and they had later outgrown him, if death and infidelity could be forms of growth. He sighed; well, that was all behind him now. He perked up as the car swung into the driveway of the largest home he was ever going to live in again.

The building stretched a whole city block, three floors for him to roam around in, even though he would occupy only a small piece of it.

The welcoming party was at the main doors and a ribbon and balloons blocked off the side door of the brand new wing. A sign above it said – "The Arnold Bradley Wing of the All Souls Nursing Home" – his last bequest and entrance ticket. Old women in wheel chairs sat in the sun – a new crop of girlfriends to choose from. The idea amused him.

A white uniformed woman, the head nurse, stepped forward and opened the limo door. "Welcome, Mr. Bradley – we thought you were not coming today. My, you have messed your clothes. We'll soon fix that. Do you want to freshen up before we go through the opening ceremonies?"

"Just a minute. I have to pay my driver." Arnold staggered around to Pervez's door. Pervez was already out, his hands crossed in front, bowing respectfully.

"Here's a bonus." He stuffed a wad of notes in Pervez's hands. "Enjoy with your wife."

"Thank you sir. You are very kind."

"Not always, Pervez – not always. Have a happy retirement some day."

"You too, sir" As Arnold turned away, he glimpsed Pervez nodding profusely and sliding back into the limo. Quietly, it slipped away.

Suddenly Arnold was tired, even though he knew there were formalities to conclude. He faced the nurse and the welcoming party again. "I'd like to lie down a bit first. I've had a hectic morning."

"Certainly. Shall we have the residents come back in an hour? There is a newspaper reporter too – we'll send him to the director's office for a while. Come with me, Mr. Bradley – let me show you to your room."

He stopped her. "Can I use a wheelchair? I've done an awful lot of walking today."

"Of course." A wheelchair promptly appeared, wheeled over by one of the many attendants standing by in the welcoming group. *Gee, it's nice to be looked after like this. Perhaps it's not all bad.*

As Arnold rolled through the doors, with the nurse pushing him, and curious onlookers staring at their new benefactor and fellow resident, he faced the one fear he'd been suppressing all morning – entering his final home, alone.

10

In the Cemetery

I met her in the cemetery in the light of morning. I have come here with increased regularity of late. I feel compelled to walk among the gravestones, reading inscriptions; many tell stories – noble, tragic or unexpected – while their subjects repose below ground, amidst harmonious surroundings, at peace, finally.

I sat on a bench a respectable distance away and watched. She wore a white chiffon dress that fluttered in the cool summer breeze. Occasionally, she tossed her blond hair so it caught the wind and billowed like a sail. Her back was turned toward me as she tended a recently dug grave. Unsettled mounds of earth and fresh flowers set it off from the others. Even though I could not see her face, the grace with which she bent over the grave was arresting, her hands gently caressing the gravestone, wiping off dust with her fingertips.

When she had carefully arranged the flowers around the site, she lay on the grass beside it, the shade from a maple tree casting her feet in shadow. She adjusted a scarf to shield her face from the sun, and very soon looked to be asleep. There was no one else in the cemetery. I couldn't resist going over.

She opened her eyes, sensing my presence, and sat up. She stared at me for awhile; our eyes locked. Blue luminosity, the absence of fear, then emerging acceptance preceded a smile.

"Hello," I said. "Nice day."

She looked around her. "Yes it is, isn't it?"

I pointed at the grave. "Close relative?"

"Very close."

I read the newly cut marble headstone. *Andrea Antoinette Fairley, left us suddenly on March 25th 2005. May she rest with the angels, for she earned heaven on earth.*

"I'm Andrew," I said.

She hesitated. "Annie," she said, extending a slim hand; it was warm and moist in mine. I sensed I could sit next to her all day and she wouldn't mind.

"Can I pass the time here for a few minutes?" I asked, sitting on the grass beside her.

"Yes – if you like. Why do you come here?"

"The peace, I guess. I feel a connection here."

"I feel the same."

"Andrea's gravestone message might describe the story of my life."

"Do you want to talk about it?" Her blue eyes were open, inviting, coaxing me on.

"I haven't talked much. Although they say it's easier with strangers."

"And I am a stranger – to you." She laughed.

But I was reluctant; I got up. "I'd like to take a walk instead."

"I'll accompany you, if you don't mind. It's a nice day for a walk." She began putting her things into a cloth satchel that she slung over her shoulder. "There are some interesting stories on the gravestones. I spend a lot of time reading them."

"Me too."

The cemetery covered several acres and was the oldest and most prestigious in the city. What had once been Jewish, WASP and Catholic-dominated was encroached upon by sections of newer Greek, Chinese and South Asian graves, some even more elaborate than their Judeo-Christian forbears.

"Those ones are interesting," Annie pointed to three adjacent graves, set back from the familiar rows by the footpath. "The grandmother, Mrs. Smith, died the same day as her two granddaughters, aged two and four."

"Indeed!" The two smaller graves were on either side of Mrs. Smith's.

"They died in a house fire." Annie said.

"How do you know?"

"Call it intuition."

I did not press her for an explanation. The Greek grave nearby also caught my attention; three generations of Kotsopouloses buried in it – Stephanos aged one hundred and two years, Alexander aged eighty and Nikos aged fifty-five – all dead within a ten-year span, the youngest dying first.

"It's hard to lose a child," she said, placing some flowers from her satchel on the Kotsopoulos grave. "Andrea did."

"So did I" I said reluctantly, and bit my tongue.

She looked at me quickly. "You do feel okay now – talking to a stranger?"

I shook my head. "Not yet. That was a slip."

"Andrea's husband was a drunk. She fell for his vulnerability.

And he beat her constantly – once, when she was four months pregnant with their only child. She miscarried."

We walked in silence – her words tore through me.

"I drank too," I said. "But only to forget."

"The memory of your dead child?"

"Children."

"I'm sorry."

"Can I see you another time? I can't talk any more today."

"I come here every morning – you'll find me beside Andrea's grave."

"I'll see you tomorrow, then."

I had to turn back and look at her from the cemetery gate. She waved to me. Never before had I experienced such concern and kindness.

*   *   *

The next day, she was painting by Andrea's grave; an easel propped up, paints strewn around her.

"Hello Andrew!" She brushed the hair from her forehead and looked up at me.

"That's a horrible scene!" I gasped. The painting was so incongruous with the beautiful painter and the lazy scenery around us. A car was plunging off a bridge; the driver, a woman pressed against the windshield, her expression a contrast of grim effort to wrest control of the wheel and horrified acceptance. A man stood on the bridge, hands reaching out as if to stop the plummeting automobile. My temples began to throb.

"Andrea's last moments." She said. "I'm trying to capture what it must have felt like."

"Her face is the focus of the portrait."

"Yes, that's what I've been trying to portray"

"What a dreadful scene. You are a great painter." The buildings in the background, the street scene, were all rendered in perfect balance, with the plummeting car and its occupant in the centre, a hole in the ordered fabric of civic life.

"Thank you." She put her brush down, stood back from the easel, looked at the picture, then at me, then back at the picture and said. "It's beginning to take shape. I like to view my subjects from the outside."

"I did not know you were working today. I thought we could walk by the gravestones and talk," I said.

"Are you ready to talk?"

"Maybe. We'll see."

She started to put her things away. She placed the easel and the canvas behind the gravestone. "We can pick these up later."

She took my hand firmly and headed south, towards the Catholic section.

I was familiar with this area. Carol and Johnny were buried here.

"You've been in this part of the cemetery before, haven't you?" she said.

"Yes."

"Tell me a story from here," she said. I steered her away from the children's graves. I could not suppress the tears and hoped she would not notice.

"Well," I began reluctantly, and then decided to let it all out. What the hell!

"Well," I said again, "There was this young couple. They married early, madly infatuated with each other, arts graduates straight out of university. Lots of pot and sex... you know."

"Uh, huh."

"The guy was a musician and a writer. She was a dancer."

"I bet they were poor."

"They were. He managed a gig at a club three nights a week, and the rest of the time he waited tables in the same joint. He was writing the great Canadian novel, but would never finish it at the rate he was going - snatches written in between breaks, losing pages when he smoked up excessively. She did a cabaret at the club but was always auditioning for the National Ballet. They lived in a rat-infested bed-sitter."

"Sounds like the usual rags-to-riches story. At least, the 'rags' part of it."

"Unfortunately there were no riches, although the sex was always good in those days." I found it easier to talk now. I held her hand tightly. She was like a life-jacket keeping me from sinking into the depths.

"She came home one day, overjoyed. She'd earned a spot with the National Ballet after three years of trying. I drank a lot and we celebrated that night in desperate release, throwing caution and condoms to the winds. Six weeks later she discovered she was pregnant and, being raised Catholic, could not think of an abortion. That blew her chances with the Ballet, and ushered in clinical depression that dogs her to this day."

We circled a sycamore tree and arrived at the twin graves by the street wall.

I sat on the grass by the graves. Annie sat a few paces behind me. I couldn't stop talking now.

"The depression got worse. Once, she tried to kill herself before the baby was born. I was drunk that night, as things had gotten out of control. She popped a bunch of pain killers and a friend, who'd been keeping an eye on us, dropped by and rushed her to the hospital, while I buried my face in a bath of cold water."

I had to stop now; the memory flooding back was making me shake.

Annie filled the void by taking over the conversation. "Andrea's husband suffered from depression. She put up with it, believing he would eventually get better." She looked at the graves, reading the stones, names, dates of birth and death. "Are these your children?"

"Yes. Carol, the eldest, was still-born."

"I can imagine. What happened to Johnny?"

"When my wife returned from the hospital, I went on the wagon, determined to do a better job the next time. I quit the club – booze and drugs were too easily available there. Got a job in a second hand bookshop. Spent more time writing my novel. In fact, I finished a first draft, but I wasn't happy with it – I was a long way from becoming a novelist. She went back to trying out for auditions at the National Ballet. But after a two-year lapse, one falls behind. She never danced with the same intensity again."

"And you never played music again either?" Annie enquired, an eyebrow raised.

"But I had my writing – my remaining artistic outlet. She had nothing, and her depression got worse." I had to get up and walk.

Annie kept two steps behind me. "You still haven't told me what happened to Johnny." Her words followed me.

"I'm getting there!" I said, almost shouting. She immediately caught up with me and took my hand, and I felt better.

"Johnny followed a year later. Both of us were trying hard to erase the memory of Carol – wanting to do it right. In her lucid moments, at least, she too, wanted to do it right. I think it's in our genetic makeup."

"Thank God for that!"

I stopped walking and faced her. My hands reached around her waist and she yielded to me. "Annie – can we stop talking about bad things? I'll tell you about Johnny another time. Just hold me for once."

"Sorry I asked," she whispered. Then she kissed me, lips warm, soothing, relaxing. My anger rapidly subsided. I sensed people walking by on the path, but no one paid attention to us, nor we to them. There we stood, in a cemetery – two souls finding comfort. Nothing else mattered.

*　*　*

The summer seemed never to end. Every time I met Annie, there was sunshine. The cemetery became our haunt. We walked among the graves, unearthing more stories from gravestones, picturing them happening in the different eras they spanned – from the mid nineteenth century to the Great Depression, during the two world wars, even to times as recent as the previous week. Everyone died in the end, no matter how progressed our civilization was. I started to feel better.

One day, she had her easel out again. This time she was working on a portrait of a young woman. I recognized Andrea, sans the terrified look.

"She must be your twin." I said, observing the remarkable likeness. Annie kept painting; delicately playing with the shadow she was giving the cheeks of her subject. "And you don't even have a photograph to go from," I persisted.

"I know her well," Annie said.

"Where shall we walk today?"

"Let's not walk. Let's talk. I want to tell you about Andrea."

I kissed her lightly perspiring forehead. The salt, mixed with her earthiness, was delicious, or was I imagining it? I sat on the grass beside her.

"Andrea was a painter. She taught art in high school. Her students adored her paintings and they loved her because she loved to teach them. 'If I can mine one gem out of all the stuff these children paint, my work is done,' she would say. And there were many gems she unearthed. So many, that she held an exhibition of the best paintings from her students over the five years she taught at Flamer High. Those paintings still adorn the walls of the school."

"What did her husband do for a living?"

"Oh, him? He was a layabout. A charming, gambling, drinking layabout. Finally, she could no longer take the binge drinking, the womanizing, the excuses. So she left him. This is how she would have looked, after she left. Unfortunately, she did not live long enough to experience her freedom."

"She met with the accident?"

"The day she left, he was drinking heavily. When he saw her loading the suitcases into the car, he roused himself from his stupor and tried to stop her. Before long, they were rolling on the driveway, biting and kicking. For the first time, she struck back, and because he was so buzzed, was able to free herself.

"She got in the car, relieved, aggrieved and mourning the departure all in one. She found the driving hard – rain was pelting down and the wind was strong. She had difficulty breathing; her husband had knocked in one of her ribs. When she got to the McLintock Bridge, she swerved to avoid a pedestrian who had stepped off the walkway as if signalling for a ride – on a bridge of all places, stupid man. Must have been another drunk. Her car hit the guardrail at such a speed, it broke through and plunged into the river below. They said she died on impact."

This time it was my turn to hold her; her body was stiff. She had applied a disproportionate overlay of shadow on Andrea's forehead, making the figure look old and in pain. I held her until she relaxed. "We'll have to redo the painting tomorrow," she said.

*   *   *

Things were starting to become clearer to me now. Our talks in the park, Annie and Andrea, their lives, mine – I felt these all as components of a higher purpose. I also realized that this idyllic time would soon pass.

We were lying on the grass in a quieter part of the cemetery. Earlier that evening Annie had completed the painting of Andrea, and they looked beautiful – both painter and subject. We had just finished making love – the first time had been the day she told me how Andrea died. On that occasion I was holding her so tightly, the fires from our bodies ignited and the next thing we knew, we were rolling on the grass, desperately clinging to each other for solace, comfort, pleasure – all those things that bring two beings together in the act of lovemaking. I had never experienced this in all my days of married life. Sex had been a physical act, nothing more; and after my wife's depression and the loss of the children, something to shy away from.

Now we made love regularly, every time we met in quiet parts of the grounds where we would not be discovered. The nights were the best in a cemetery, although occasionally teenagers sneaked in to try it out themselves, just for kicks. Those who could see us would probably think we couldn't feel those emotions at our stage of life, but then, none of them were where we were, yet. I couldn't get enough of Annie. Surrendering completely to her and knowing I was safe; that there would be no accusations of being a drunk and an errant father. There was only acceptance for who I was in that moment. We also talked a lot and came to realize how our lives had intersected. Sometimes we would go on for hours, until the sunlight broke through, or the birds began chirping.

"Andrea looks beautiful in the painting," I said. "The contours of her face, her expression. She looks a lot like you. And there is an inner radiance in her eyes that is just dazzling."

"It took a long time," she replied.

"I love you," I said, turning on my side and kissing her ear.

She kissed me back. "I've waited all my life to meet someone like you too, Andrew. It seems perfectly natural, what we do here."

"Like being in the Garden of Eden."

"Yes. But you know it's going to end now, don't you?"

"Yes. I am preparing for it."

"You still did not tell me about Johnny."

"Ah, yes, Johnny." I was scared to tell her about Johnny. I wanted to prolong our meetings in the cemetery. "Can't we do it some other time?"

"There is no time, Andrew," she said rising. "Take me back to Johnny's grave. Perhaps then you will remember."

As we went over to the Catholic section, memories returned to me.

"Johnny was born with a weak heart, a year after my mother passed away. He was also allergic to everything under the sun – milk, dust, pollen, wet wood, penicillin, cold weather, hot weather – I forget what else. My wife blamed herself and slumped even deeper into depression. It was her cop-out, like booze had once been mine. She beat the child when she ran out of options to care for him. I had to take time off work to look after him when he was sick, because I could not trust her with him. My employer wasn't happy either, especially since I had already taken leave earlier to care for my mother."

"Johnny was too good for this polluted world," Annie said.

"That's one way of looking at it. On Johnny's fifth birthday, I lost my job at the bookshop – for taking all that time off, I guess – although they would not say why. Just gave me notice and three weeks pay."

"Some people don't know how to be kind," Annie said. Her words spurred me on.

"I broke my promise that day – fell off the wagon. Drank from morning 'til late afternoon, 'til most of the three weeks' pay was gone. When my wife saw me coming home, she called me a no-good drunk, grabbed Johnny and made to leave the house. I tried to stop her, begging for forgiveness, but I was so hammered.

"I remember stumbling after her, down the stairs of our apartment. She let go of Johnny to take a swing at me. My boy fell down three flights and broke his neck. The police took her away on manslaughter charges. They locked me in the slammer too, until they concluded that I had not pushed either of them."

I was exhausted and we had reached the children's graves. I sat down. I couldn't speak anymore.

Annie took my hand. She kissed the side of my cheek and I realized how wet my face was. "I know how you must have felt. This talking has been good for both of us."

Then she rose and began walking away from me, and I knew that I would never see her again. I followed her to the cemetery gate, where she paused and turned around. "I only remember driving recklessly that day, holding my damaged side. There was a complete void afterwards that I was hoping to recapture. Thanks for helping me piece it together."

"Why did you wait so long? Why did you not leave the day you spoilt Andrea's portrait?"

"I waited for you. Watching you come to terms helped me do the same. It helped me restore Andrea to her true self."

Then she was gone and I knew it was useless to go after her. All I now had were the memories she had left behind, the sweetest ones I had retained in my entire life. All that was left of her was a faint glow that could have been coming off the street lights. After a while the glow dimmed, betrayed by the coming dawn.

There was one more part of the cemetery I needed to visit; a part I had steered away from since first arriving here; an older part of the Catholic section where my parents were buried. I went over to the family grave.

The duller inscriptions were still visible in the moonlight.

Douglas James -born 1930, died 1980, suddenly taken away to God (heart attack, I barely knew my father).

Mona James – born 1931, died 1999, died in peace with God (cancer, God bless her soul, she fought hard to live).

Below, was a fresher, more elaborate one: *Andrew James, only child of Douglas and Mona, born 1966, died tragically March 25th 2005*

Today, I felt vindicated. I was able to relive the day I burned my great Canadian novel in the realization that it was never going to be published, the day they let me out of jail and cleared me of my son's accidental death. I could now relive the rush of river water as I jumped off the bridge, uncaring for my own life, but desperate to save that of the woman who had gone over in the car to avoid a drunk and staggering me who had been celebrating the burning of his manuscript. Nor was I any longer afraid of the memory of the slimy liquid gushing into my lungs, as the strong current swept me downstream so far, that when the cops found my body, they would not have connected me with the dead woman.

Yes, it was time to let go, to accept the change and move on. I bowed my head over the James family grave; hovered and waited for the light that had taken Annie to return for me.

11

Let My People Stay!

The Rev. Julia Styles looked out from the rectory and across the road towards St. John's. It was a beautiful spring morning and the grove of sugar maples under the old matriarch tree shading the front entrance would soon be in bloom. In no time, her church would be returning to nature and become worthy of its name again – St. John's-among-the- Maples. Beneath its large, new neon sign the caption, "All Christians are welcome," echoed the beliefs of its founding fathers from fifty-five years ago. On Sundays, the parade of Mercedes and BMW's will arrive with the Chinese service goers. The poorer ones will come via public transport, or on foot, for the outdoor service under the large tent that has taken up the entire old parking lot — and they come from all over now, even as far as the lakeshore. It seemed like only yesterday when getting newcomers, let alone younger people to come to Sunday service had been an uphill battle. Now you couldn't keep them away. God had indeed willed it, and she was happy for this.

She took the little white tablets out of the bottle; she needed more of them now just to keep that demon of pain at bay. Swallowing them down and steadying herself, she put on the 'nature' chasuble made by the children, over her white alb. It was covered in prints of trees from all over the world, which the children had hand painted – from maples, to akee trees, to bamboo shoots. Today was also her special day, her day of reckoning, she knew. Her mind went back disjointedly to the events that had led to this pass. It had all started about five years ago.

*   *   *

"We can't run like this anymore – it's all deficits," Marion Derby, the senior warden and treasurer said. "The Women's Auxiliary is in deficit, the Sunday school is without a teacher, the building is in need of repairs and our weekly intake is less than our expenses."

It was the annual general membership meeting, and Rev. Julia looked among the audience of regulars. Old Joe Smiley sat in the same seat he had occupied when she was still a teenager. His wife had passed away the previous year and the man was going downhill fast; he even had an oxygen tank and tubes in his nostrils. The number of canes and walkers had gradually increased and Julia was glad for the investment they had made in the elevator soon after she took over as pastor from Rev. Morris six years prior to this very day. It had drained the building fund but at least these folks could get around inside the church now – including going to the hall downstairs for coffee after service, and to other social celebrations that kept this community together.

Harry Bailey, retired high school teacher and former warden, piped up, "I didn't hear that clearly – my hearing aid's acting up. Why the devil are we in deficit? We ran our affairs so well all these years. I would think the new wardens need to get their act together."

Here it comes, thought Julia, the same old factional bickering – a disease that spread among this aging population faster than the cancers and strokes that were killing them off steadily. But then, old people do get cranky, she reminded herself.

"Just a moment, Harry," Julia said. "It's not a question of the wardens not doing their job. We saw the aging of this community years ago. We have not been successful in bringing new people to the church. Now we are paying a price."

"People who would come to this church have left the area – moved to the burbs – Ajax, Whitby and the like" someone piped up from the back row.

"There are only them immigrant types now," Joe wheezed through his oxygen tubes. "I got two of 'em on either side of my house – oriental looking."

"Maybe we haven't been inclusive enough," Julia said, knowing this would provoke a reaction.

"Wha'd'ya mean?" Maggie Kendrick, head of the Women's Auxiliary jumped up. "They came to this country – they gotta play by our rules – isn't that right?"

There were hesitant "yeas" in the room. Five years ago, when Julia had suggested a multicultural service the "nays" from this group had been louder. There had been more of them too, now many were dead, and the rest were not so sure.

Marion Derby brought the gavel down. "All this debate is well and good, but we don't have all evening. So here are our options. We can either wind up matters – that is "die with dignity" as our church leaders say, or we can partner, amalgamate, join – whatever you want to call it – with another church."

"You have a third option." Julia whispered in Marion's ear.

"Yes, as Julia here reminded me, we have an offer from the local Christian Chinese Association, the CCA, to hold their services in our church. Their start-up donation alone will wipe out a big chunk of our debt."

A dead silence descended on the room as everyone digested this bit of information.

Then Maggie steamed up again, "And they'll turn this place into something unrecognizable. Soon we'll be burning joss sticks."

"Getting rid of the debt is not a bad idea," Harry said. Then he shrugged. "On the other hand, I don't know. Maybe, as Maggie says, it's not a good thing after all. We've always managed without outsiders."

"They'll stop us from coming to service!" Joe wheezed. "I know; they never talk to me. Every time I say 'good morning' they nod and run indoors."

"Maybe your neighbours don't understand English very well, Joe," Julia said. "Folks, I know this is a lot to deal with. Why don't you reflect on this? Pray on it and ask God for guidance. We have some tough choices ahead of us."

* * *

Two months later, Julia walked among the maples in the evening twilight and reflected on that day's events. The proposal to accept the CCA, made by the wardens that morning, had been ratified by the congregation at a special general meeting. It had not been an easy event and there had been a lot of soul searching and angst.

St. John's needed the money, no question, and its members had agreed reluctantly – some even shedding a few tears. Following the vote, Julia made the call herself that afternoon on Mr. Charles Wang, president of the association, at his offices in Agincourt where he ran a trading company.

Mr. Wang was a slight man of fifty-five, with thinning grey hair and large glasses. He was dressed in a suit. He rose from his desk, bowed and shook hands with his guest. Julia towered over his five foot-nothing height. He kept craning his chin upward making his neck seem longer than normal. He fussed about ordering a clerk to bring tea, coffee or anything that the priest wanted, all of which Julia politely refused. Finally she settled on a glass of water, just so she would not offend him.

"Ah, Rev. Styles – that is good news. At last we have our church."

His office was adorned with large rattan chairs, porcelain jugs reaching above her head and large paintings depicting the years of the Chinese calendar. But interspersed in all this ethnicity were photographs of the queen, the prime minister of Canada and the Toronto Maple Leafs. Outside the office, clerks and other employees rushed back and forth speaking animatedly in Mandarin.

"Mr. Wang. May I ask you a question?"

"Certainly." Mr. Wang beamed.

"Most of your community is in this area and there are many churches here that offer service in your language, why are you coming down to our side of town?"

"Ah, but yours is the area where the regular Canadians live. We must be there. Not in our little box, no?"

"You call this area your box?"

"Well – you see, it is like this – one Chinese person comes, then he brings another, because he has no one here. Then they bring others. Very soon we have so many of our own kind to talk to and we don't need anyone from outside. But all the time our children are going to Canadian schools and don't like their parents 'ghetto' – yes, that is the word?"

"So you are trying to get out of your ghetto?"

"It is a great privilege for us." Mr. Wang beamed again. "More water?"

"No thank you. I must be going. As I mentioned our service is at ten o'clock in the morning. You can have yours in the afternoon."

"Afternoon very good for us – everyone will come. And we can also use the hall?"

Julia hesitated. "Well the hall wasn't part of the deal – but if it's not in use by one of our various committees, you can have it. Give us plenty of notice. The Building committee would also appreciate a donation for the use of the facility which goes towards its maintenance."

"Ah, no problem. Money is no matter – we will pay. You won't have any more financial problems now."

Julia began to flush. Is this how Judas felt when he received the thirty pieces of silver? But this was not just her doing – the membership had spoken. She was merely the messenger. She shrugged off her feeling of guilt. "I wasn't thinking purely of money, Mr. Wang. The building needs upkeep."

Mr. Wang deftly rose from behind his huge desk and came over, took her hand and escorted her to the door. "Thank you Rev. Styles – this is a big day for us."

Now she walked in the fading twilight among the maples and

wondered if they had done the right thing. St. John's was certainly going to change radically. But wasn't change part of growth?

She remembered when her father Jack had returned from the war – when all the men in the neighbourhood had returned. She was about ten then. The men had been silent, some stayed in their homes all day; others went to the hospital regularly to have various missing limbs and injuries treated. Jack hadn't been hurt, but his tone towards her mother changed; he snapped often and went out drinking with the guys every weekend. Julia would often go down to the garden in Old Bailey's dairy, and pray under the maple trees. The suburbs were filling up, there were no more spaces to pray in the old churches built before the war; there was also no church in her fast growing sub-division. Those moments of prayer were better than any of the formal services she had ever attended. She would strum tunes like "The Garden" and "My Cathedral" on her guitar as she sat and meditated under the trees. One Sunday morning, her father returning home from a night on the town with his pals, found her deep in prayer under the giant sugar maple and suddenly grabbed her hand and said, "Honey, the diocese agrees – we are going to build ourselves a church."

That day he stopped his carousing, got the men rounded up and they converted the old dairy into a church, helped by a grant of land from old Mr. Bailey himself, who had lost both his sons in the war. The men volunteered their time, working night and day and on weekends while the women kept the food lines coming. To the men it was just like a battle, and they went about it with grim purpose. She remembered her father issuing orders through his megaphone as he surveyed the construction. She had never seen him more animated since his return from the war. St. John's-in-the-Maples was built in three months. At the opening ceremony, her father squeezed her hand and said, "Julie, remember you must always have a purpose – it gives you reason to go on." Two months later, with the church fully operational and the men returning to their normal activities, including her father to his weekend binges, Jack Styles blew his brains out with his hunting rifle and the community was shocked, but the men only nodded grimly.

She prayed for guidance after that. Her mother became depressed and would stay in her room for hours, while Julia cooked, studied and generally tried to keep the whole show going. And she played her guitar and prayed when the emotional load got too heavy. At eighteen and on the cusp of entering university to take a degree in divinity, she met Rob – a handsome, rather rakish engineering grad with a red sports car. She remembered nights at the movies, Rob driving like a maniac along Kingston Road, the night they made love up on the bluffs. He had given her a trillium that day. Even to this day she maintained a trillium bed in the church garden, which the children were forbidden to touch. The night of her graduation, Rob asked her to marry him. She prayed to God for answers. Was this the right thing to do? She never got a chance to answer him. That night after the graduation dinner, with a little more to drink than usual, Rob drove his red sportster into a tractor trailer and died on the spot. She survived the crash and was left with her evening gown stained in his blood and the divine answer she had been looking for. The next month Julia enrolled in divinity school.

The fifties, and even into the late sixties were great times to be a priest. Churches were booming. Children filled Sunday school classes; there were christenings and confirmations by the dozen and people religiously came to service because there was really nothing else to do in this city on the Lord's Day. The formality and spiritual rush she felt when celebrating the Eucharist was intoxicating. No wonder priests felt so different from mere mortals. Yet she missed those quiet moments of meditation among the maples when she had felt nearer to God than when in front of hundreds of people chanting hymns during a regular Sunday service.

During that period, Julia moved from church to church all over the province, doing four or five-year stints at each stop, always coming into a new community with lots of determination to make a difference, always leaving with tears over the many hearts and souls she had touched and changed. In the mid seventies, when her mother became ill with the cancer that had taken many of her family, Julia got a position as assistant to Rev. Morris at St. John's so she could be near to her only living relative.

Walking now under the maples, she remembered how the neighbourhood's demographics had slowly changed. It started soon after her mother died. The war generation started moving out as they became empty-nesters in the early eighties – down to cottage country or elsewhere out of the clutches of Toronto. The new entrants were immigrants from all over – China, the Caribbean, India, Sri Lanka and the Middle East. These were people unfamiliar to her, but the children were sweet; they spoke English or picked it up quickly in school. But there was no Christian religious instruction in the public school system now, so how could she attract these new families to church? Many of them already had other religions. The only thing in common appeared to be the struggle they all underwent as newcomers to this country; trying to hook onto career paths, climbing social ladders and making economic progress. Providing counsel to immigrants on these subjects was, unfortunately, outside her mandate or experience.

Even the suburban bungalow-style housing, so characteristic of her community, began to change. Because of the immigrant influx, re-zoning had led to high rise apartment complexes springing up around the parish. Emerging from the maple grove and looking skywards she saw the lights from these new structures. One particularly large apartment building just across the street, was about to be completed this summer; it was twelve stories high and nearly a block across and its shadow darkened the parking lot that had always been so sunny. Dust from its construction was constantly in the yard. On his first visit to St. John's, Mr. Wang had seen and approved, "Good – just like Hong Kong – lots of construction – sign of health."

* * *

"They've strung up a big Chinese sign and it's covering our notice board!" Maggie Kendrick came storming into the minister's office one Saturday afternoon as Julia was preparing her sermon.

"It's for their service tomorrow. Mr. Wang asked my permission."

"But no one will see our special service information."

"Be serious Maggie – who does anyway? That board is so obscurely placed; no one drives out here just to read it. I'm sorry to sound negative, but that is the truth. And what's wrong with sharing our church with people who want to worship – even if it's in their format?"

"My God – have you become one of them? Has their money gotten to you too?"

"No – I'm simply trying to be charitable."

Maggie grunted and sat down. She fussed about with her papers. Then she got up and paced.

"Something bothering you, Maggie?"

"It's George – he's not doing too well again."

"Oh, you should have told me. Do you want me to come over?"

"No – it's all right. I have to manage haven't I? All the others – Marion, Agatha, Phyllis – they all lost theirs, didn't they?"

"Shall I put his name down in our 'prayers for the people' section? At least, we can pray for him."

Maggie came closer and there were tears in her normally feisty eyes. "I'm scared this time, Julia. I can feel it – he's not gonna pull through."

Julia rose and embraced Maggie. The woman was trembling. "Now, now – you know, we are always with you."

"Is that what dying with dignity means?"

"What?"

"What they said the other day – that we are all dying off, and all this church is doing is seeing us off to the hereafter before shutting its doors."

Embracing this dear parishioner who had given so much of her life and time to this church, Julia was unable to respond. She merely held Maggie closer.

*   *   *

"Mr. Wang, I cannot agree to this. You know my parishioners have been attending the ten o'clock service for decades. They will not settle for an afternoon service."

"But afternoon not convenient for my people – many working now because of Sunday shopping. Your people are retired, no?"

"That's not the issue."

"We have too many protestations in our association about afternoon service now. Maybe we will have to move to another location. But we like your location. Would you please reconsider?"

Julia paced her office. Her guest sat silently watching her every movement.

"Well – I will put it to the committee. This will not be an easy decision for them."

"Much financial risk for you, if they say 'no', no?" He rose and bowed. "Make decision soon. We can't wait."

*　*　*

"What's next? We gave them the hall, gave them the morning service, now they want to be on our committee?" Maggie Kendrick was livid. George had just passed away two weeks earlier, and she was still in deep grieving.

"Well – they are now contributing about sixty five percent of the finances – for the first time this year we have a surplus to help with outreach," Marion Derby said, peering over the ledgers, trying to remain neutral.

"They're gonna take us over." Joe Smiley said wheezing and gasping for air through his oxygen tubes.

"We can't always have them on the outside," Julia said. "As demanding as they are at times, they have a right to be included."

"But they will soon discontinue our services." Harry Bailey said, "That's what they'll do. It's all about money with them. All those auctions and donations and stuff going on here. Never seen that in my time."

"Come now Harry", Julia said. "Your generation built this church. My dad was one of your buddies. You had fund-raising then too; we've all done it at one time or other. We just haven't been successful in recent times, while the CCA has."

"But not like this – a hundred dollars for a ticket to their anniversary dinner?"

Marion Derby cleared her throat. "If I can bring you folks back to the point we are discussing – Mr. Wang has asked to be represented on our governance committee."

"And I say 'no'!" Maggie Kendrick erupted.

Julia went over to her and put her arm around her, and the older woman burst into tears.

"Oh, well – let 'em in." Harry said in disgust. "Let 'em in and let's be done with it. This place is not what it used to be, anyway."

"This place is changing Harry," Julia looked up from tending to Maggie. "The war changed you men permanently. Now we have to be open to the changes in our neighbourhood."

"I wish I could go somewhere else – up to Keswick or somewhere. But I can't afford it anymore." Harry banged his walking stick on the floor.

After further debate and a downwardly spiralling argument to exclude the CCA, a vote was taken and Mr. Wang got his place on the committee.

* * *

One day, she tried standing in front of the newly opened apartment building across the road – Halton Towers – handing out flyers about St. John's and inviting the new residents to come and worship. Passers-by extended hands mechanically and took the brightly coloured leaflets, but no one looked excitedly at the "good news" in them. They seemed pre-occupied with the work of putting bread on the table, juggling jobs and minding kids – the daily struggle of new immigrants starting at ground zero. A young woman with two children in tow was staring at her. In between her distribution activities, Julia observed her closely. She looked like a Tamil, dark long hair, thinly built; she was wearing a cross and chain.

"Hello – I'm Julia Styles from St. John's."

"I know."

"Oh"

"My husband and I came and looked at your service once – very traditional, no? We couldn't follow. And the Chinese service too, but we can't understand their language."

"You've been to St. John's?"

"We were at back of church. People were staring. We are not used. Another priest was saying the mass."

"Oh, that must have been Reverend Gillies, my back-up – I must have been on a retreat. Will you come again?"

"I like to. But my husband very shy."

"What service did you have in your native country?"

"We are from northern Sri Lanka. Our church was burnt in the war. We prayed in the open or in our homes sometimes."

"Are you happy here?"

"Not like back home but better – no killing, at least. My family all killed. Mother, father, two brothers. All killed." The woman was resolute in her delivery as if she were talking about the weather. But Julia realized that this young woman had the maturity she too had attained at a young age – a maturity that comes with intense and tragic loss.

"Will you try and come out at least one more time? We need people like you."

The woman averted her eyes. Then she pulled the hand of the toddler and made to go indoors. "I will try."

"What is your name?"

"Mira. Mira Kandasamy."

"God go with you Mira."

Mira smiled and a faint playfulness exuded. "God is with me, even though I don't come to your church. He led me out of hell in Sri Lanka. And saved my children also."

Then pushing the little boy ahead of her and carrying the infant, she went through the front doors and was swallowed up in the building.

*　*　*

"You, what?" Rev. Julia Styles was aghast. The proposal from Mr. Wang and his cohorts – who were now the majority on the governance committee of St. John's – was shocking. Cancelling the afternoon English service because it had fallen below the mandatory twenty-five attendees required!

"Afternoon service too expensive. Not enough donations. Have to spend far more on heating, electricity etc. etc., especially during winter." Mr. Wang had a determined look on his face – something she had begun to see in recent times.

"But this is our church. We built it!"

"No longer – now everyone's church – your people and mine – especially more Chinese people now."

"So what alternative do you propose?"

"Your people can come to either morning service or afternoon service. Both in Mandarin, I'm afraid – but we sing English hymns."

"That's not going to work. We don't understand your language."

"And many of my people not comfortable with yours. They struggle with it in business and at work; even their children speak to them in English and make them feel like strangers – they need to come to church to feel at home again. Very difficult to get out of the ghetto all at once, only very slowly. Their church, very important to them."

"You wouldn't have done this if we hadn't got you on the board."

"But you did – now many of your board members are dead – so who will carry burden, eh?"

Julia grimaced – it was true. They'd had four deaths and one serious illness on the board in the last twelve months, so the Chinese had stepped in. And things were running better too. But the loss of their Sunday afternoon service? Unthinkable!

"Why don't you come to our service and see?" Mr. Wang said. "Not too different than yours – English hymns."

"It is different. I came and saw the last time – your visiting minister is a stranger to my parishioners, the format is unrecognizable, the traditions are unfamiliar. It's not the same."

"That's what we felt when we first came to this country. That's why we need our own service."

Julia rose. There was no further use talking. "Mr. Wang, I think I made a big mistake inviting you into our community. We tried to build bridges between cultures – to include you. But you are excluding us. We may be dying out, but we are not gone yet. I am asking you one more time; will you let my people stay and have what they were used to?"

"Impossible financially. That is my final answer."

"We shall see – as God is my witness, and I do not mean to be acrimonious, but we will not be forced back into our homes. I know what it was growing up without a church. We will fight back, if necessary."

"Wish you all the best. After you finish fighting, you can always come to Sunday morning or afternoon service." Mr. Wang turned away and busied himself on the computer.

Julia stormed out of the church office. Outside, Halton Towers loomed down on her. Clothes hung on lines and junk filled the balconies. Soon it would be just another dirty, cramped apartment building.

"Help me, dear God," she said looking skywards. "Give me a sign that will help my people stay and die with dignity. A sign that will see this church grow in tolerance and love again."

A full bus disgorged a number of passengers outside Halton Towers and tired workers trudged up the walkway to the building. Inside, blinds were open in many of the apartments. She could see people moving about – children studying or playing in cramped quarters, adults moving tiredly after a long day's work.

She waved at Mira Kandasamy who was sitting on the balcony with her children, looking anxiously at the bus stop, waiting perhaps for her breadwinner husband to come home. In another apartment, a couple was arguing; their hands waved furiously as the children remained glued to the TV. Where was God in their lives? Or had they temporarily forgotten Him because they had so much ground to recover since coming to Canada? Or were the avenues to God – churches like St. John's with their insulated traditions – closed to them?

Then it hit her. *They* too must be looking for a sign to come into the fold, to be included. And all this time she had been looking for one only for herself and her dying flock!

*   *   *

"Are you crazy?" the normally calm Marion Derby exclaimed. "The weather is cooling now; people are going to catch their death outside."

"Not if there is warmth in their hearts," Rev Julia Styles was arranging the plastic chairs – hauled from the church hall in the basement – in rows on the front lawn. She had managed to bring out the full contingent of thirty chairs; they probably would not need any more. She had personally called each member to inform them that despite the notice last Sunday from the governance committee informing that future afternoon English services were discontinued, she, Julia Styles, was conducting a "special service" and would they all come? And bring some warm clothing along too. She had left Marion for last, her sense of realism telling her that she would put a damper on it.

"Will you help me bring the table out, Marion?" The older woman looked perplexed, but nodded and followed Julia back into the basement. They struggled, but got the table out on to the lawn

Julia placed a white altar cloth on the table, pinning its edges down in case the wind picked up. Then she placed her prayer book, a loaf of fresh bread bought from the supermarket, carafes of wine and water, a bowl and a cloth. She had borrowed two braziers from the foundry at the top of the road, and filled them with briquettes that she would light when the gathering was assembled. And she had her guitar handy, knowing old Harry Bailey would strum. He missed a few chords these days, but they would all follow anyway.

"What the devil is going on Julia?" Maggie Kendrick was struggling up the walkway. She used a walking stick now and paused tentatively before stepping onto the lawn. "Is this where we are having our new service?"

"Maggie – please take a seat, and enjoy," was all Julia could say as she busied herself with the arrangements. She had wind-proofed the candles by placing glass dollar-store cylinders around them.

Slowly, the old parishioners began to arrive; some even went up the church steps before figuring out that the action was taking place on the lawn instead. There were many questions, but Marion, who had got the general drift by now, turned chief usher and explained what was taking place, as she herded the new arrivals to their seats. CCA members were arriving too, and they looked with amusement at the growing gathering outside as they entered the cosier confines of the sanctuary for their new afternoon service, about to start at the same time.

"Good on ya, Julia," Joe said taking his seat on one of the plastic chairs and resting his oxygen container on another.

Mr. Wang came hurrying over, dressed in a dark blue suit with a bright yellow tie, his hair, slicked back and shiny. "Rev Styles, what is happening here?"

"We are merely having our service, Mr. Wang. Nothing to be bothered about. And we will not interrupt yours. You can shut the front door."

"But we get in trouble with the municipality, no – if too much noise outside?"

"Then we will deal with it when that happens. We can't be thrown in jail for worshiping our God, Mr. Wang. This is Canada, after all. And this is not 'noise'. Now if you will excuse me …"

Seeing the determined look on the priest's face, he shook his head and retreated. At the door he threw one more barb, "We will have problems, I tell you – and then you will be responsible."

"God go with you Mr. Wang."

When Julia, fully garbed for the service, looked at her congregation, there were muted smiles and uplifted faces. They normally grumbled; today that was all gone, replaced by a feeling of pride. George took the guitar and strummed "Oh, Canada" which surprised everyone but they sang it with gusto. People in the street, stopped and watched, some even stood to attention during the national anthem. Blinds were being drawn in the windows in Halton Towers, when Julia stepped forward to address the audience with her father's old construction megaphone, which still miraculously worked, having needed only a new battery.

"My dear friends – today we begin our new life in this community as worshippers in the way Christ taught us – out in the fields, in the open, subject to the elements. We will break bread as

He did; not indulge in pre-packaged wafers. We were once like that, in the days before this church was built. But we got cozy and insulated. Others who have followed us, and espouse the values we pursued, have also gotten cozy and insulated." She paused and the organ sounded inside the church, accompanying an English hymn sung by accented voices. "And most of all – we will not be relegated to praying in the isolation of our homes. This is a community, and we will keep it together until the last one of us is gone.

"As we get older and return to the Lord, it is time to return to innocence, to nature and I invite you all to pray for everyone in this community, both inside the church and outside, so that St. John's will go on, no matter what. You will notice that for today's service, all the long prayers are gone. Today we will pray as God taught us – with our hearts and minds, and in the words that come to us in that state of grace."

Joe cackled in the front row. "Let's show 'em, Julia. If Jesus himself did it on the Mount of Olives, heck, why can't we do it here, eh?"

"This is not a competition, Joe. This is our quest for God, no matter what or where."

The prayers came easily after that. They all prayed in a stream of consciousness, the jumble of voices sounding almost as if it were in tongues; but all together they emanated like a serene and heavenly buzz. The hymns were "Across the Bridge" and "I'll Fly Away", but not "God Save the Queen". When she raised the chalice during the consecration of the Eucharist (the only formal part of the service) Julia saw many blinds drawn fully open in the windows of Halton Towers. Mira Kandasamy was on the balcony and her toddler was holding a candle in his hands. Even the quarrelling couple was standing side-by-side inside their window, intently watching the service. And Mr. Wang had come outside and was slowly shaking his head.

When the service ended sooner than customary (thanks to the trimming of the eulogies and antiquated hymns), the congregation dispersed, gratefully shaking Julia's hand and thanking her. Yes, they would come again, despite the cold – it had been good for the soul, they said. Uplifted, Julia packed away her things to take indoors. She felt a presence and turned around. Mira was standing there, shrouded in an oversize coat. Her children were also bundled up.

"Thank you – we like your service. We understood it."

"You did? Will you come the next time?"

"I'd like to. And I will also tell others."

"What others?"

"Our people. Many are praying in motel rooms on Kingston Road. God helped my family get out of there. But the others are still waiting for His help. I think He has sent you to help them."

* * *

"Okay, okay – so I make a shed in the parking lot for your service before winter," said Mr. Wang. He was pacing inside his office. "With heaters."

"And you will get the necessary municipal permit for shifting our car park to the office building on Dorset Road."

"But too many people now on the lawn. Need to control crowds."

"God is in control, Mr. Wang – there is no need to control anything."

"But people from building next door are also on lawn now."

"And it's about time too. They needed to see God in action, not in the confines of a mono-cultural church. They saw, and now they have come. I would advise you not to follow the path we followed – or one day your numbers will also diminish."

For the first time, she saw the little man look worried.

"Okay, okay," he said and continued pacing.

Yes, that was how it had all panned out, the turn of the screw. The "lawn service" became an outdoor service and ran right into the winter, before the shed and heaters arrived to improve conditions. And many came from near and far, and the midnight mass on Christmas Eve even blocked the road. Police had to divert traffic but no one complained. Complementing Julia's small group of aging parishioners on the lawn were Indians, West Indians, Sri Lankans, East Europeans – they all came, mostly from Halton Towers, donning parkas and mitts, wanting to be a part of this community, which had suddenly lost its exclusivity. The service was simple and non-intimidating. One prayed in the language one was familiar with. Even the regulars did not complain that Julia had cut out the longer prayers and readings, since they couldn't stay out long in the bitter cold. They wanted only the essence, and were grateful for the fact that they still had the opportunity to pray together. Maggie Kendrick summed it one day when she hugged a West Indian child who had come with his parents: "Julia, when one is as close to dying, as I am, it's just nice to be surrounded by people – even if they are strangers."

And Julia knew that her life's intent had manifested itself when the next annual budget showed that the outdoor service on a stand-alone basis was not only covering its costs, but also contributing to the general coffers of St. John's and its outreach work. At the elections for wardens, one new warden was elected to counterbalance the incumbents Marion Derby, Mr. Wang, his cousin, Mr. Low and their cousin, Mr. Lee. The new warden-elect was Joseph Mbako, the man who had been quarrelling with his wife just months earlier. He was now a regular attendee at the outdoor service. Mr. Wang looked relieved – "Ha, now we are multi-cultural, no? Now you won't give me any more hard times eh, Rev. Styles?"

The Woman's Auxiliary took off as well. There were events almost every other week. Mira Kandasamy ran the daycare so people could once again drop off their kids when coming to service, something that St. John's hadn't seen since the late seventies. Julia was awash in activity herself, overseeing the myriad church committees that were springing to life again; helping her older members pass on; assisting the revived youth group with Bible study; inducting members who kept coming, as word of mouth spread among the newcomers, trying to learn the new customs and languages. She was even teaching spoken English to some of the new arrivals. Joe Smiley passed away that year, smiling and happy as he had always been. Harry Bailey had a stroke and was confined to a wheelchair in the nursing home. Even when she started having the first pains in her breast, Julia focused on integrating newcomers into her expanding church. After all, that pain had gotten most of her family and it was her turn now, but there was still so much work to be done, and suddenly much less time to do it in. She increased her workload at the church and tried not to think of the growing lump.

*　*　*

"You are going to say mass, today? It's only Wednesday." Mira Kandasamy said, her two kids in tow. She came in during the week to clean the rectory, now that Julia was having difficulty most mornings, especially after the morphine took hold.

"No – I just wanted to feel good – feel that my life has been useful. Wearing these garments is a measure of my worth. Like a general wearing his military uniform and medals in public." Julia said, and sat down, exhausted. The pills were taking affect and her near- permanent grimace was easing. Cramped face muscles relaxed. It was a relief to let go.

"You should not exert yourself now, Reverend."

"Oh, Mira – I'd rather be dead than still. Here, help me onto my chair and push me across the road to the maple grove. I need to sit in the sun under the trees today."

With Mira pushing and the kids running ahead, they crossed the road to the church. The shed, soon to become a permanent extension of the church when construction began next month, loomed huge – it now housed more than seventy-five people and had outgrown its purpose. Its replacement would still maintain the concept of a "garden" with large indoor plants, a glass ceiling and a sandy central area with altar and pews running around it – Julia had designed it herself. The main building was sporting a new coat of paint and Mr. Wang had sprung for the neon sign and a taller steeple that rose above most buildings in the area. People were coming and going from the church – various committee members – even on this weekday. The new pastor, Rev. Jason Lee – fully bilingual in English and Mandarin- was talking to a couple of Women's Auxiliary members at the front door. St. John's was alive and bustling.

"Do you want me to stay here with you?" Mira asked respectfully bending down.

"No Mira – please take the children with you – you have work to do. I'll be all right."

"Are you sure?" Mira's dark eyes showed concern but also understanding.

Rev. Julia Styles smiled. "Yes, my child – I am with God now, just like He has always been with you. Get on with your work."

As the young woman hurried back across the road, Julia smiled and raised her head heavenward.

"Reverend Styles –" the voice was tentative.

Through a haze she saw the slicked back hair, the suit and the neck no longer straining upwards but looking down at her in the wheelchair.

"Mr. Wang!"

"I bought you small gift." He stretched out a hand holding a huge bouquet of flowers.

"Thank you Mr. Wang. Put them by the trilliums for now. Later you can put them at the altar. And come and sit by me in the sunshine."

The Asian flowers, anthuriams and orchids, looked vibrant next to the trilliums.

"St. John's growing church now, eh?"

"Yes – it's just like Canada, Mr. Wang."

"Yes – like Canada."

Mr. Wang sat by her in the maple grove for a long time – until time itself did not matter to her anymore.

12

Silence

I drove out of the city into open farmland, past new subdivisions sprouting up intermittently and biting into nature, until the road ended at St. Joseph's. "Drive to the front gate and wait," said the instructions on the web site. So I waited, not for long. The gates slowly creaked open. I inched the car along the driveway, among tall maples, cedars and oaks dotting the rambling grounds of the monastery, to the parking lot. In the fading light and drizzle, I hauled my bag containing two changes of clothing, enough for Friday evening to Sunday afternoon, and followed the arrows for newcomers.

Silence helps one come to terms. That was the promise of St. Joseph's and the premise on which I came this weekend. Since Angela's death, all I had done was go to work and go home, forcing myself to *do* – not to think. When deadlines began to slip and I found myself staring out the office window at traffic, as work started becoming increasingly meaningless, and John, my boss, came by one day and said, "Andy, you need some time for yourself; it's showing", I decided to do something radical. Grief counsellors, medical doctors and family had done all they could; the pain had gone to depths greater than any of these folks could plumb. When I punched in the words "grieving", "enlightenment" and "forgiveness" on the Internet, they led me to St. Joseph's website.

Silence was not what I found as I pushed through the doors at the reception. About forty men sat or stood in small groups at various locations in the large reception hall, talking loudly, some even hurriedly. A fireplace at the far end promised respite from the damp November weather. A thin sixtyish man with a sallow complexion sat at a table drawn across the entrance. He had some papers before him.

"Hi, I'm Joe," the man greeted me with a smile, revealing crooked, stained teeth. "Welcome to St. Joseph's."

"My name is Andrew David."

"Ah yes. Here is your key and welcome kit. Your room is in the west wing. Chimes will ring for each session. The rooms are singles, and showers are across the hall of each wing. Meals are served in the main house across the grounds. Relax, have a cup of tea or coffee, and meet the rest of the retreatants. The chimes for silence go off in about twenty minutes."

I tried to retain all that information amidst the background chatter. I put down my bag in a corner and got my bearings. Several bookracks were located at various parts of the reception hall, with a cash box beside each. Purchases were on the honour system. I browsed some of the books nearby – Christian literature, all of them – plenty of Mother Teresa, the Fatima apparitions, Padre Pio, and various how-to books on applying Christian principles to secular life. A tiny kitchen with coffee, tea and snacks ran off to the right of the fireplace. Doorways leading to the east and west wings, housing the bedrooms, faced each other midway in the reception hall.

The men ran a bell curve of ages from forty to eighty. I picked up the last available stool in the room and walked over to a group huddled in armchairs by the fireplace.

"Hi, I'm Andy," I said plunking the stool down and sitting on it. My fellow retreatants looked me over, smiling, appraising, some even appeared annoyed at the disturbance of their ramblings. Two overweight red-faced men, who introduced themselves as Ted and Bob, were the loudest and the jolliest, constantly joking, always with an anecdote to enliven the conversation. I gathered before long that they were recovered alcoholics. Two Filipino's in the group looked scared. The older, whose name I soon learned was Oscar, kept muttering instructions to the younger one, Angelo, who acquiesced each time. Even though Angelo was almost double the size of the older man, he seemed to be in fear and awe of Oscar. I turned around to survey the group again. That's when I saw the old man.

He sat alone by one of the bookracks with his chair up against the wall. His complexion was pale, his eyes closed; he breathed in short rasps. He must have been in his seventies, a big, emaciated frame with clothes hanging off him. Only his full head of silvery hair indicated what must once have been a handsome specimen of White Anglo- Saxon Catholicism.

Chimes rang and silence descended. The veterans of previous retreats (and I later discovered that many had been coming here for years) rose, threw their styrofoam cups into the garbage and headed down the southern hallway. The old man got up shakily and Joe was immediately at his side to assist.

I heard the old man say in a hoarse voice that hit a few falsetto notes, "It's okay, Joe. I gotta do this last one on my own."

I followed the procession of men down the hallway to the chapel at its end. We sat in the semi-circle of pews and the priest conducting the ceremonies, a fleshy bald man with a cherub face, introduced himself as Fr. McKay.

"Gentlemen, and this time there are no ladies, welcome to St. Joseph's. I see many familiar faces, and also many new ones. Over the next couple of days you will deal in silence with the issues that have brought you here. The Holy Spirit will be with you. The Spirit appears in strange ways on these grounds. Remember, silence stills the mind. Silence shuts out the chatter that constantly surrounds and blinds us to insights from the Spirit."

Fr. McKay took us through some prayer meditations that we could use, if we chose, to help us on our spiritual journey. He ended the lecture with the Lord's Prayer.

"Good luck, gentlemen. I will be around for the daily lesson and the nightly Eucharistic celebration. If you need counsel from either me, or my colleague Fr. Anselm, please write your name on the appointment sheet on the bulletin board as you leave. God Bless you all."

*   *   *

Silence is disquieting – when you suddenly begin to notice the flickering of the light bulb in your room and anticipate the next fluctuation; when the sound of raindrops on the window becomes loud and relentless; when you want to talk out aloud to yourself; when you can't wait to turn on your laptop and do e-mails; when you know that all these things are not possible because you have taken an oath to still the mind, to remain silent except at prayer times. When you are therefore, looking forward to the next prayer time, you've come to know the fearsome isolation of silence.

In the adjacent room, the old man coughed violently through the night. Each hack ended in an eerie whine. My bed creaked with every toss or turn. I tried to focus on the furnishings for the umpteenth time – no TV, no telephones - just a desk, some prayer materials, a tiny cupboard, and a washbasin and toilet in a closet, and, oh – a creaky bed.

I tried to go through the prayer routines Fr. McKay had given us, but my mind was distracted. Angela flitted in and out of my thoughts, as she did most nights. What was it she wanted to tell me? That I had missed the significant events in our lives: like the children's university graduations, Tammy's skating performance at the regionals, Jeremy's theatre debut at Stratford? I shifted in the squeaky bed. I knew that horrible scene would play out again – Angela in the hospital with the sheet drawn over her; me trailing my travel bag, leaning over her bed and feeling guilty because I had not said goodbye.

The old man coughed again. I rose from the bed and went out into the darkened corridor to get a glass of water from the kitchen. His door was ajar and a tiny night lamp illuminated him seated at the desk, bundled in a blanket. He was using the prayer sheets. His face had a pleading quality. Then it struck me – this was the same expression I had seen on Angela's face when I pulled the sheet back that day in the hospital, an expression that said, "Lord, I don't want to go so soon."

*   *   *

I awoke the following morning after a restless night. I longed for my own bed; travelling as much as I did, it was a luxury. I walked into the reception hall and found a few retreatants in corners, individually now, as silence was in observance. I got myself a coffee from the kitchen, pulled up a chair by the fireplace and watched my companions filter in.

Ted and Bob arrived together whispering, which sounded clamorous in the prevailing silence. Annoyed stares from the others quickly silenced them. Ted and Bob made a beeline for the coffee, then slumped into deep armchairs and buried themselves in magazines. Through the large windows I saw retreatants walking about the grounds in the early morning mist, heads bowed, rosary beads dangling from hands.

I closed my eyes. Only the movement of people came to my ears. The silence had completely taken over. Yet, my mind could not focus. I tried the prayer routine in my head. Halfway into it, I sensed someone sit down next to me. I opened my eyes, losing the faint thread of concentration just beginning to take hold. It was the old man. Dressed in a heavy sweater and denims, he looked worse than when I had seen him on the two previous occasions. His jaw was set firmly, as if he was determined to see this retreat through. Instinctively, I opened my mouth to enquire about his cough and then held back – of course, silence had to be observed. He looked at me and smiled, his sunken cheeks lightening for a brief moment, cavernous eyes seeing something I could not.

The chimes rang for breakfast and we filed out across the

grounds to the main building. The dining room was airy and spacious with tables for six and a buffet at one end. We piled our trays in silence with good wholesome food – bacon, eggs, hash browns, cereal, juices and fruit. We ate in silence too, each intent on his thoughts. For once, I was relaxed; I did not have to make small talk, like I did on business trips, often not eating most of what I had on my plate, and feeling hungry afterwards.

Two lay-person staff, both women, replenished the buffet from the kitchen. The younger one, blonde, curvy – and subtly flaunting it, I thought – caught my attention. All the men, regardless of age, were gawking. I was glad Fr. McKay had not arrived yet, or I would have felt ashamed. Despite our issues, we men hadn't forgotten how to lust, it seemed. I had not indulged in carnality since Angela passed; guilt always got in the way. When I went to return my tray, the younger woman passed by and smiled coquettishly. Her name badge read "Nella." For the brief instance our eyes locked, I could feel the power she wielded over me – I could look, but not speak, and she could flaunt and tease as much as she wished.

After breakfast, I walked the grounds. Nature trails extended in various directions. The one I took led to a large circle in the middle of a field. The circle was called the Labyrinth, a maze of concentric pathways, cut into ankle-deep grass, connected to each other, moving you down to the core, then swinging you off to the other side and towards the periphery, then bringing you in once again, and so on. After a while, I knew I was never going to get to the centre. It made me think of Angela – of how we argued in circles over our relationship going nowhere in the later years, after the children left home. I had to be either wedded to my job or to her. For my part, we had a family because of my job; it gave us the house in Richmond Hill, the two cars, put the children through university and bought the cottage, cash down. Angela loved the cottage – she'd disappear there for the whole summer. Sometimes I thought she did that just to get away from me and my constant work patterns. She also scanned the help wanted ads, cutting out various job postings. What she did with them I never knew.

That fateful day, six months ago, I had been at the company sales conference in Palm Springs. Returning after a very satisfying round of golf during our R&R period, the message tucked under the door in my hotel room simply read, "Call home – urgent." There was no reply when I called. Despite being fraternal twins, Tammy and Jeremy lived in different parts of the country now. I tried both their cell phones and left messages. I left another message on the home answering machine and waited to hear back. That night was the sales gala banquet, which I could not miss. The cell phone in my pocket rang, but I did not hear it during the speeches and applause – I was on stage most of the evening, dolling out awards to sixty needy sales people. When I got to my room after a final nightcap in the bar with the team, my cell phone showed three attempts from a number I did not recognize. The kids had left messages too, enquiring what the matter was, and more importantly – why was I calling out of the blue? I called the unrecognizable number first. It was the North York General Hospital. Angela had suffered a brain aneurysm and collapsed at the bookshop and was in critical condition. I phoned the twins back and let them know; they were naturally distraught and I offered to pay for trips home if they could get out of their various commitments. I could not get a flight back until the morning. When I arrived in Toronto the following evening, it was too late.

Who had called and left the message, "Call Home – urgent?" And why the hell had I not reacted faster?

I walked back to the retreat quarters. As I passed the parking lot, strains of music leaked through the half-open windows of a van. Ted and Bob sat inside, chatting and smoking. When they saw me, they looked startled. I smiled and made to continue on my way, when Ted rolled down his window and whispered, "Come here."

I went over to the van and would have broken my silence unwittingly when Bob put his finger to his mouth and said, "Shh! No sense in you breaking the spell too. We need to. We are party boys, always were."

"Yeah that's what got us into trouble in the first place," Ted muttered. "Where there's a party, there's booze."

"Don't worry, brother," Bob said. "There's no booze here. We can manage that, but we can't get by without the music. The silence just kills us."

I nodded.

"Oh no, you don't know where we'd be if we didn't come here regularly," Ted said.

"Back in AA, that's what," his companion whispered. "Or dead drunk."

"We've been coming here four times a year since Bob and I came out of rehab. Ten years in a row, eh, Bob?"

"Eleven."

"Now, don't go telling Fr. McKay that we're out here breaking the code of silence, okay, brother?" Ted had a pleading look in his eyes, eyes that had lost their colour a long time ago from too much alcohol, eyes trying hard to regain their lustre.

I nodded again and returned to the retreat centre.

* * *

I made an appointment to see Fr. McKay at two o'clock that afternoon and went into the refectory and lit a five-dollar candle for Angela. The flame would last for five days the notice over the collection box said. I stared into its light, hoping to see her. She always got to the heart of the matter, raking up the difficult issues we business types skimmed over. Spending more time in the office than at home, my communication style with Angela had a distinctly corporate flavour, she used to tell me – non-confrontational, diplomatic, tactful. That's what got you ahead in the professional world – not necessarily at home. I recalled our argument just before my departure to Palm Springs.

"I'll call you when I get to the hotel," I had said, lugging my travel bag to the front door, slinging a sweater over my shoulder – a useless thing once I disembarked on the other side.

"Don't bother," she replied from the kitchen. "I will be working."

"You… you've got a job?"

"Surprised?"

"Where?"

"Wordsmith's Second Hand Bookstore. Ten dollars an hour."

"Should you, honey? You haven't been back to work for five years. And with your blood pressure …"

"Oh, bugger that. You always find something to hold me back. First the kids, then your career to support, now my health. Are you embarrassed that I will ruin your professional image?"

"But you don't have to work." I heard something smash in the kitchen and thought it better to pursue this subject another time. "Anyway, I'll call you from Palm Springs and we can discuss it then."

Angela, fiery Scorpio, loving mother, never really achieved her aspirations as a writer – how could she, with Harry Potter sucking up everyone's money? Who had the time for a wannabe literary fiction writer of lyrical prose, who had wasted her best creative years supporting a corporate executive and two over-achieving children?

The chimes at St. Joseph' rang for lunch and dragged my thoughts back to the present. The silence was helping. Since her death, these were the most continuous thoughts I had retained of my wife.

Lunch was difficult. My stomach churned. It must have been all those thoughts of Angela. What would I have given to be sitting on a beach, playing golf, dining in fine restaurants, doing all the things I was accustomed to as a businessman, avoiding the cold hard facts of life? Instead, here I was with a bunch of silent men, facing reality, huddled over bland, but nourishing food. Even ogling Nella did not help.

*　　*　　*

"We left things unfinished." Fr. McKay and I were sitting across from each other in his private quarters, a small living room lined with bookshelves and containing two lounge chairs and a small coffee table. It was nice to talk again; yet I felt that I was cheating by breaking the silence that had induced the flashbacks.

"Life is inconclusive," said Fr. McKay. His eyes were gentle. I did not feel so alone anymore.

"She phoned that morning before going in to work. But I was playing golf. She must have sensed something was about to happen."

"It's easy to blame ourselves for what could have been different. Better to accept what occurred, and move on."

"We all want to be successful in life – in business, and as husbands and fathers."

Fr. McKay just smiled. "If Jesus had thought like you, he would have thought his entire life had been a failure when he was stuck up on that cross."

*　*　*

I saw the white cat later that afternoon. It was about three o'clock and I had taken another nature trail skirting the boundary of the property. On the other side lay monster homes, on land sold to developers by the monastery as its finances had worsened. I had looked up the area on the old map in the common dining room at lunchtime. Each house had a pool that peeped through the wooden fence separating the new residential area from the residual Church property. The weather had turned wet and cold again, a thin drizzle making the pathway soggy, the fallen leaves turning to mulch beneath my boots.

The path branched off from a straight line of pine trees on either side into slight hills where the undergrowth had crept over. I had to push young branches aside to make my way forward in certain places. There was no one in sight; I had passed the last retreatants several minutes ago – Oscar saying his rosary at the entrance to the trail, with Angelo right beside him. I wondered if the old man was mustering his courage and praying for divine help to undertake the trek.

The white cat caught me by surprise as I rounded a bend onto a clearer section of the trail. She was right in the middle of the path, frozen in stillness, looking straight at me. Fr. McKay's words, "The Holy Spirit appears in strange ways on these grounds," immediately came to mind and I stopped in my tracks. We stared at each other across ten yards of pathway. I shook my hands thinking it would follow my movements. It did not budge. Was it an illusion? A statue placed there by someone to trick me? A bee buzzed into the cat's space and I saw the twitching of its whiskers, so I discarded the last thought.

Why was I afraid? Perhaps it was the direct stare of the creature boring into my soul, the silence, the damp, the falling light and my unstable mood – a potent cocktail that made the cat look more like a ghost with every passing moment. Should I throw a stone at it, shoo it away, or take another route to avoid confrontation? I looked around. Behind me the path branched downhill through a thicket of trees in the direction of the monastery. I stepped back. The cat stayed immobile. I inched onto the second path. The cat just stared, probing, unearthing, condemning.

I walked faster than usual, the hairs on my neck standing up in the damp, fearing what I would see if I turned back. Then my fear got the better of me, and I ran. Breaking branches that swung into my face, I kept going until I came through the trees and into the open field, the Labyrinth on the right, the way back to the monastery clearly in front of me. I looked over my shoulder. The cat had not followed me. I slowed to a fast walk, goose bumps all over, feeling foolish and cowed. I had been scared... by a cat!

Angela would look at me like that cat. That was it! I turned around, I had to face this. I crept back through the trees, heart in my mouth. I was going to return to that cat, pick it up and pet it, fondle it, caress it even – do all the things to it that I had not done to Angela. Holy Spirit indeed!

But when I arrived at the spot, the animal was gone. I called after it, walked in circles around the area. I even peeked through the fence at the large house on the other side, thinking the animal belonged there.

No cat.

Disappointed, I turned back and headed towards the monastery in the thickening drizzle to the sound of the chimes, signalling time for the way-of-the-cross.

*   *   *

"We normally conduct the way-of-the-cross at the stations marked around the grounds." Fr. McKay pointed through the stained glass window of the chapel out into the yard that was taking a steady downpour. "But given today's inclement weather, we will conduct it indoors around the chapel."

"Why can't we go outside?" one of the retreatants asked. "Jesus had no comfort when he did the first one."

A loud chorus of agreement rippled through the group. We were gluttons, masochists; and given the mood I was in, I wanted to take my share of whipping – or drenching.

Fr. Mackay shrugged and reached for his umbrella beside the altar. "Okay then, gentlemen. Please file outside – and bring your raincoats."

We huddled under the first station. The fourteen stations ran around the large front quadrangle of the grounds at fifteen yard intervals, zigzagging between the giant oaks and maples. Bob held the heavy brass cross; Ted distributed prayer sheets, while the veterans took turns leading the group at each station.

"Wait for us!" Joe ran out, pushing the old man in a wheel chair, the latter draped in a transparent plastic wrap.

Fr. McKay paused, and went over to the old man. "Are you sure you can manage this? It's going to be awfully wet."

The old man's look was steely. "Of course, I can," he wheezed.

Joe shrugged, and Fr. McKay nodded and returned to his hymnal, suppressing a smile.

Despite my raincoat, I was soaked by the fifth station; at the tenth, my teeth began chattering, but only if I thought about it. It's amazing how physical discomfort allows one to focus outside the body. In my mind, the seeds of concentration that the silence of the last twenty-four hours had planted, finally took root. My focus was not on the rain, but on letting go, letting someone else take charge; just as Jesus did before he succumbed. *Father, into thy hands I commend my spirit.* It was a great release. And watching the determined group of wet humanity around me was comforting. The old man had been well waterproofed by Joe; but he occasionally peeked through the covers, raising his head toward the heavens, letting the rainwater pour down his face as he smiled at some unseen entity. The arrival of thunder and lightening somewhere during our journey around the stations, completed the scene.

As we broke at the final station, the presence of wet and cold came back sharply. The bolts of thunder had changed from a distant rumble to periodic cracks, and lightening streaked down just outside the monastery gates. We trudged back in clumps towards the retreat centre, Joe wheeling the old man buried in his makeshift plastic tent with a hand upheld in a victory sign, Oscar holding Angelo's shoulder under an umbrella, others running for cover or absorbed in their thoughts and oblivious to the thunderstorm.

I felt a tap on my shoulder. "This will warm you up." Fr. McKay slipped me a hip flask. "You are not dressed for this weather."

I looked around, embarrassed. Fr. McKay winked. "The brandy will do you good. I wouldn't offer it to everyone here though," he said, looking around furtively, but Ted and Bob were engrossed in stowing their way-of–the-cross paraphernalia. I gratefully took a couple of swigs and let the spirit warm my insides.

*　*　*

That night, after the thunderstorm ceased, I thought the old man had died. There was no coughing, no stirring… nothing. I wasn't in a mood to go exploring; my throat was starting to get sore. I had asked for it. But my spirit felt good. I had to perform some act of courage after running away from a cat. Well, I had done it, and now I had to wear my badge of honour, a cold.

I forced myself to get up and tiptoed into the darkened

corridor. As usual, the old man's door was slightly open. He was propped up on his bed, breathing evenly, a night lamp full on his face. He had not been at dinner or at the evening's Eucharistic celebration and I had begun to wonder. But now he seemed to be at peace, sleeping soundly. I was about to step back, when he stirred and opened his eyes, their gaze gripping me.

Before I could speak, he raised emaciated fingers to his lips in a silent "Shh!" I remained silent and looked apologetic for my intrusion. He crooked his finger, beckoning me into the room. I advanced tentatively, until I was at his side. He bent his finger again and I leaned over.

"It's okay," he whispered. His breath was tinged with the scent of some medication. "Once you get over the fear, its okay."

I held his hand and wished it was Angela's. Yet at that moment it was a good proxy.

"Go back to sleep, young man. Remember – once you get over the fear, it's okay."

I tiptoed back to my room.

* * *

The following morning, we trickled into the reception hall, grabbed tea or coffee and took our familiar seats in various parts of the room. The drill was familiar, the silence welcome, comforting. My nose was stuffed up, but there was a lightness in me; the kind that comes when you realize that the things you did instinctively, wrong though they may have been at the time, were the best your soul would allow you under the circumstances.

Angela was not coming back. Our relationship had not been the happiest, was inconclusive during its run, and ended that way too. Perhaps, in writing this down and sharing it with someone else, the children maybe – I could help someone avoid the same mistakes. And for a healthy fifty-four-year old, who said that there was no possibility of starting over again? Where had these answers come from? Just through a good night's rest?

After our solitary breakfast, the Eucharistic celebration was dedicated to prayers for special needs or loved ones. For the first time I listened to retreatants say their petitions out publicly, breaking the silence with their own words.

I was surprised at how many were grieving for lost spouses, parents, even children. I was not alone. I just thought I was. I petitioned aloud for the soul of Angela. Amidst the company I was in, it was now easy to do. I had never done anything like this in a church before, always preferring to pray in silence. My corporate reticence to disclose the personal had stifled me until today. Fr. McKay, dressed in full regalia to celebrate mass, nodded in approval; my fellow retreatants replied, "Lord, hear our prayer," with gusto.

Oscar was the only one with an unusual petition. "Lord. Keep my family safe in the Philippines, my wife Magdalena and beautiful daughter Eva. And bring them safely to Canada, quickly." At least, his prayers were for the living.

*   *   *

"Oscar was kidnapped for ransom back home," Angelo said. We were at the final lunch, the chimes had sounded, permitting the

200

silence to be permanently broken and everyone was talking again, the sound at a pitch similar to when I first arrived at the monastery. Oscar and Angelo, Ted and Bob, the old man and I were at one table.

The old man looked up from his plate at Angelo's comments and nodded knowingly. Oscar, Ted and Bob were still getting their food from the buffet.

"Is that why he lives in fear?" the old man asked.

"Yes. I am his son," Angelo replied. "He doesn't let me out of his sight."

"He needs to come out here more often," the old man said. Oscar arrived at the table followed by Ted and Bob. Suddenly it felt crowded; yet all that had changed from prior meals was that we could talk.

"Well, fellahs – how was it?" Ted said heartily, mapping out what to eat first on his plate. Bob had already begun tucking in.

"The silence was a new experience for me," I volunteered. "Normally, I am always talking."

"Yep. Aren't we all?" Bob said, between mouthfuls.

"The silence reminds me of when I was blindfolded for five days," Oscar said.

Bob and Ted looked surprised and I tried to clarify by aiming my response into the middle of the table, "We know about your kidnapping."

While Angelo explained to the bemused ex-alcoholics, Oscar continued, "When Angelo and his friends rescued me, they brought me to a monastery outside Manila. That's where I found refuge."

"You must have a lot of money," the old man said, moving the leftovers to the side of his plate and laying down his cutlery.

"I sold everything after my rescue. I gave most of the money to that monastery. My wife and daughter are still under their protection until they can come to Canada."

"Then why are you afraid?" the old man said, pushing back his plate.

Oscar looked down at his food. He hadn't touched any. "I think my kidnappers are still trying to get me."

"You need to come here more often," the old man said, placing his napkin on the table and rising slowly.

*　*　*

The sun had come out, but the air remained chilly. We were leaving the monastery; retreatants stowing their baggage, the veterans hugging each other, promising to meet again next year, cars driving through the gates. Going back to our daily lives, where silence would be hard to maintain, let alone find.

As I went out to my vehicle, I saw the old man sitting on a bench just inside the doors. I stopped and held out my hand.

"It was nice meeting you. I'm Andy."

"Jim. Did you find what you came looking for?"

"I found some."

"That's a start. I've been coming here for five years now, ever since I was diagnosed. I only got my answers yesterday. Then there was no more fear."

"Will I see you the next time?"

"I don't think so. I might not make it that long. But there is no need for me to come again either."

"Goodbye then, Jim."

"Farewell Andy. I hope you find your answers."

I left him there, head resting back, a half-smile on his face. A man ready for the next part of his soul's journey. He was indeed a good surrogate for Angela.

As my car neared the front gates, I saw Nella standing on the left, waving at the vehicles heading out. Looking at her blond hair in the sunlight, voluptuous breasts thrusting through a tight sweater, a wave of desire coursed through me; something I had not felt since Angela's passing – lust, maybe; desire, never.

But what got my heart thumping was when she bent down and picked up something, held it to her breast and stroked it gently, in between waving at the departing retreatants. I was mesmerized by the soft white fur that coursed through her fingers, at the twitching of whiskers in satisfied acquiescence. Nearing, I rolled down the window.

"Thanks you for your hospitality, Nella," I said.

Her wide eyes twinkled. "You're welcome. Do come again."

"That's a nice cat you have there. I saw it on the trail yesterday. Can I pet it?"

"Sure."

She held out the animal to me. I reached out and stroked its soft fur. It purred contentedly at my caressing.

Acknowledgements

I wish to thank my publisher Richard M. Grove (Tai) for his enthusiasm and support, especially over a cup of afternoon tea; and my editor Jake Hogeterp, whose eye for the errant sentence or word is uncanny, yet whose sensitivity in preserving the voice of the author is paramount.

Thanks also to my many reviewers who gave me feedback and helped me shape these stories to be worthy of publication: Nancy MacLean, Sharon Crawford and her band of readers from the East End Writers Group in Toronto, Brian Mullaly and his readers from the Pollard Group of Writers in Northumberland County, and the Canadian Authors Association's Virtual Branch members from coast to coast in Canada for their online critique. Thanks to Gail Murray for her poem Valentine Promise that spawned the story by the same name. To Federico Serrano for his photography on the front cover. To my sons Jonathan and Richard who understand Dad's time-outs for writing. And to my wife Sarah, for her unshakeable belief that I was meant to become a writer.

Shane Joseph

Author Biographical Sketch

Shane Joseph began writing as a teenager living in Sri Lanka and has never stopped. From an early surge of short stories and radio play scripts, to humorous corporate skits, travelogues, case studies and technical papers, then novels, more short stories and essays, he continues to pursue the three pages-a-day maxim and keeps writer's block at bay.

His career stints include: stage and radio actor, pop musician, encyclopaedia salesman, lathe machine operator, airline executive, travel agency manager, vice president of a global financial services company, software services salesperson, and management consultant.

Self-taught, with four degrees under his belt obtained through distance education, Shane is an avid traveller and has visited one country for every year of his life. He fondly recalls incidents during his travels as real lessons he could never have learned in school: husky driving in Finland with no training, trekking the Inca Trail in Peru through an unending rainstorm, hitch-hiking in Australia without a map, escaping a wild elephant in Zambia, and being stranded without money in Denmark, are some of his memories.

Shane is a graduate of the Humber School for Writers and studied under the mentorship of Giller Prize and Governor General's Award winning author David Adams Richards. *Redemption in Paradise*, his first novel, was published in 2004. *Fringe Dwellers* is his first collection of short stories. His latest novel *After the Flood* was released in November 2009. His short fiction has appeared in *Existere* magazine, in several Canadian anthologies and in literary magazines in India and Sri Lanka.

After immigrating (twice), raising a family, building a career, and experiencing life's many highs and lows, Shane has carved out a niche in Cobourg, Ontario with his wife Sarah, where he continues to write stories and play his guitar.

Books in the North Shore Series

Find full information at
– http://www.HiddenBrookPress.com/b-NShore.html

First set of five books

— **M.E. Csamer** – Kingston – "A Month Without Snow"
   – Prose – ISBN – 978-1-897475-87-2
— **Elizabeth Greene** – Kingston – "The Iron Shoes"
   – Poetry – ISBN – 978-1-897475-76-6
— **Richard Grove** – Brighton – "A Family Reunion"
   – Prose – ISBN – 978-1-897475-90-2
— **R.D. Roy** – Trenton – "A Pre emptive Kindness"
   – Prose – ISBN – 978-1-897475-80-3
— **Eric Winter** – Cobourg – "The Man In The Hat"
   – Poetry – ISBN – 978-1-897475-77-3

Second set of five books

— **Janet Richards** – Belleville – "Glass Skin"
   – Poetry – ISBN – 978-1-897475-01-0
— **R.D. Roy** – Trenton – "Three Cities"
   – Poetry – ISBN – 978-1-897475-96-4
— **Wayne Schlepp** – Cobourg – "The Darker Edges of the Sky"
   – Poetry – ISBN – 978-1-897475-99-5
— **Benjamin Sheedy** – Kingston – "A Centre in Which They Breed"
   – Poetry – ISBN – 978-1-897475-98-8
— **Patricia Stone** – Peterborough – "All Things Considered"
   – Prose – ISBN – 978-1-897475-04-1

Third set of five books

— **Mark Clement** – Cobourg – "Island In the Shadow"
  – Poetry – ISBN – 978-1-897475-08-9
— **Anthony Donnelly** – Brighton – "Fishbowl Fridays"
  – Prose – ISBN – 978-1-897475-02-7
— **Chris Faiers** – Marmora – "ZenRiver Poems & Haibun"
  – Poetry – ISBN – 978-1-897475-25-6
— **Shane Joseph** – Cobourg – "Fringe Dwellers" *Second Edition*
  – Prose – ISBN – 978-1-897475-44-7
— **Deborah Panko** – Cobourg – "Somewhat Elsewhere"
  – Poetry – ISBN – 978-1-897475-13-3

Forth set of five books

— **Diane Dawber** – Bath – "Driving, Braking and Getting out to Walk"
  – Poetry – ISBN – 978-1-897475-40-9
— **Patric Gray** – Port Hope – "This Grace of Light"
  – Poetry – ISBN – 978-1-897475-34-8
— **John Pigeau** – Kingston – "The Nothing Waltz" - *Second Edition*
  – Prose – ISBN – 978-1-897475-47-8
— **Mike Johnston** – Cobourg – "Reflections Around the Sun"
  – Poetry – ISBN – 978-1-897475-38-6
— **Kathryn MacDonald** – Shannonville – "Calla & Édourd"
  – Prose – ISBN – 978-1-897475-39-3

Single Anthology

"Changing Ways" A book of prose by Cobourg area authors including:
Jean Edgar Benitz, Patricia Calder, Fran O'Hara Campbell, Leonard
D'Agostino, Shane Joseph, Brian Mullally. **Editor: Jacob Hogeterp**
— ISBN – 978-1-897475-22-5